EVIL FLOWERS

Also by Gunnhild Øyehaug

Present Tense Machine
Wait, Blink
Knots

EVIL FLOWERS

STORIES

Gunnhild Øyehaug

Translated from the Norwegian by
Kari Dickson

Farrar, Straus and Giroux
New York

Farrar, Straus and Giroux
120 Broadway, New York 10271

Feather on title page by Potapov Alexander / Shutterstock.com.
Feather on page 117 by MVelishchuk / Shutterstock.com.

Library of Congress Cataloging-in-Publication Data
Names: Øyehaug, Gunnhild, 1975– author. | Dickson, Kari, translator.
Title: Evil flowers : stories / Gunnhild Øyehaug ; translated from the
    Norwegian by Kari Dickson.
Other titles: Vonde blomar. English
Description: First American edition. | New York : Farrar, Straus and
    Giroux, 2023.
Identifiers: LCCN 2022044455 | ISBN 9780374604745 (hardcover)
Subjects: LCGFT: Short stories.
Classification: LCC PT8952.25.Y44 V6613 2023 | DDC 839.823/8—
    dc23/eng/20220916
LC record available at https://lccn.loc.gov/2022044455

Designed by Patrice Sheridan

Our books may be purchased in bulk for promotional, educational, or business
use. Please contact your local bookseller or the Macmillan Corporate and
Premium Sales Department at 1-800-221-7945, extension 5442, or by email at
MacmillanSpecialMarkets@macmillan.com.

www.fsgbooks.com
www.twitter.com/fsgbooks • www.facebook.com/fsgbooks

1   3   5   7   9   10   8   6   4   2

CONTENTS

EVIL FLOWERS

BIRDS

As I sat on the toilet menstruating, a fairly large part of my brain fell down into the toilet bowl. I'd seen brains on TV, so could easily differentiate a piece of brain from a piece of mucosa. There it was—not black and clumpy, but brownish pink and shiny. I said nothing when I went back into the kitchen, I just sat down and ate my tacos as if nothing had happened. I did a few quick checks to make sure I was still functioning—did I understand requests like "pass me the sour cream" or "can I have the taco sauce, please"? I ran through the names and ages of everyone around the table, my husband and three children, and I looked out the window to see if I still knew where I was. Then, as I chewed, I quickly estimated the dimensions of the kitchen, rattled off the alphabet in my head, ran through the lineage on my side of the family, and Tom's. Everything seemed to be in working order. But later, when I went back up to my office and sat down to work, I saw something hanging from the yellow desk light that I didn't recognize. From the way it was hanging, it must have been there for some time, it certainly wasn't new. It was a peculiar shape, a kind of half-moon, with an uneven curve and a kind of tip at one end. The tip was black. The underside was yellow and the topside a darker yellow and black, and some white with something that resembled a human eye in it, only when I looked closer, it lacked the white of an eye. Across what I would call the back of the half-moon were some cuts that looked like parallel grooves, which ran back toward the flat end. When Hans popped his head in around the door a little later, I took the thing off the lamp and held it up. Hans was ten, so might possibly know what the thing was, if he wasn't too young. What is this, Hans? I said. He looked at me, a little nervous. It's . . . it's a kind of tit, but I'm not sure what kind, please don't be angry. Angry, I said, why would I be angry? You normally get angry when I don't know exactly what kind of bird it is, or what sound it makes. Oh, I said. So what's a tit? Mommy, you're the one who can answer that, he said, exasperated, I can only tell you it's a bird! A small bird from the tit family. He threw up his hands and closed the door. So the thing in front of me was something he called a bird, from the tit family; none of it made any sense to me. I googled. "Bird." I was presented with a list of things similar to the thing that is called *bird* in the singular, *birds* in the plural. It was a living creature, and I could see that they all had that tip coming out of what I'd come to realize was their head, but the tip varied in size and shape, and was actually called a beak. And birds could fly—I had to laugh out loud when I discovered that. These were creatures that could actually fly! I heard a knock on the door. My husband stuck his head in. Hans said that you asked him what sort of tit it was, Tom said. Nina, surely there's a limit to how many categories you expect them to know, isn't it enough that they know it's a tit? Yes, of course, I said. He seemed to soften. I know that your defense is coming up, and I understand, I really do. But you can be certain that you won't be asked to classify the tit family. He came over and gave me a hug. He looked at my screen, which was full of images of different birds. He laughed. Back to basics, I see, he said, and left the room.

I noticed that there was a Word document on the toolbar. Apparently it was my thesis, as my name was on the front. It turned out that I'd written my thesis on rheumatism in the snipe family. It transpired that I was an ornithologist. I googled myself and found out that I was employed by the University of Bergen as a researcher and I was going to defend my doctoral thesis in three weeks' time. I thought about the piece of brain that I'd flushed down the toilet. It was now clear that I'd lost the part of my brain that held all my knowledge about birds. It probably goes without saying that I felt extremely anxious as I sat there at the desk. I felt

stunned, sick to the core, and scared, then suddenly one
of those creatures came flying through the air and landed
on the veranda outside my office window, and looked at me
through the glass. I laughed, I'd never seen anything like
it before. It was a black-and-white bird, and it started to
hop mischievously toward the balustrade before opening its
wings and flying off. I laughed so loudly that Tom stuck
his head back around the door, with a folded T-shirt in his
hands. What's going on? he said. I saw a black-and-white
bird out there on the veranda, I said. A black-and-white bird,
Tom said, and looked at me pensively as he put the folded
T-shirt down on a pile of already folded clothes on a chair
by the veranda door. You mean a magpie? Yes, a magpie, I
said, and felt myself blush. Nina, I think you should take
a week off, he said. Go and stay with your parents, go for
walks, relax, don't think about your defense.

And so I went home to my parents for a week. I tried to read
up on the snipe family as my father practiced Handel's *Messiah* for a Christmas concert and my mother went to meet-
ings. They tried to get me to do what Mom said Tom had told
them I should do in a secret phone call, not to think about
birds, to go out for walks, to the cinema, to eat food, to sleep.
My mother took me on several canoe trips, but I kept getting
distracted whenever a bird landed on the water, and then I

got stressed because I couldn't remember what kind of bird it was. Mom pretended that there weren't any birds, no matter what happened, not even when we went for a walk at dusk one day and spotted a plump bird, almost half a meter tall, with big round eyes, up a tree. She pretended not to see it when I pointed, busied herself with getting a bar of chocolate out of her anorak pocket, then broke off a piece and said: Here. When we got home, I overheard her telling my father that we'd seen an eagle owl, and that was a first; there had been rumors that there was an eagle owl in the area, but my mother had certainly never seen an eagle owl before. I googled "eagle owl" and saw that she was right: we had seen an eagle owl. Now, when I could no longer fully appreciate it. I hadn't even been able to place the plump and apparently very rare bird in the owl family.

One day when I was sitting at the living room table with my laptop open, Mom came up behind without me noticing, and saw what I was reading about on the internet: the snipe family. She said she'd been thinking about sorting out the family snapshots that were just lying in a box in the loft, and putting them into albums, and wondered if I wanted to help. She held up a large plastic bag with five big black photo albums in it. Of course, I said, and closed my laptop. Mom must have forgotten there were pictures from a family trip to the bird

cliffs on Runde when we were small. I held a photograph up
for Dad, and he squinted over his glasses, looked at his three
children lying on the edge of the cliff, our hair blowing in the
wind. We were laughing and smiling at the photographer.
Below us was a sheer cliff face, with thousands of tiny white
specks. What are those specks? I asked my father, as he sat
there practicing Handel's *Messiah*. Goodness, not easy to say,
really, Dad said, as though he were struggling to see. Are they
birds? I asked, pointing at a bird that was closer to us, and
recognizable as just that: a bird in the air. Yes, it could well
be, Dad said, then sighed and added that it was the cliffs at
Runde. We often went there when you were children. Hm, I
said. He stroked my cheek. It'll be fine, he said. Everything
will be fine. You don't need to worry about it. He gave me a
hug, and I shed a few tears. I didn't say that a part of my brain
had fallen out, and that I'd lost everything I'd ever known
about birds, and that I had ridiculously little time to build up
all that knowledge again in order to defend my thesis. That it
wouldn't be fine, that I would stand there like an idiot, with
only piecemeal knowledge about the snipe family.

Having read a bit about the snipe family, I could understand
why I'd become so fascinated with the bird at some point
in time. There were several different types, even the names
were interesting. For example, there were common snipes
and great snipes. As if a common me and a great me might

exist as well, I thought. I saw a picture of a great snipe on the internet, and thought that it was called a great snipe because it had two beaks, one higher up on the face and the other a bit farther down on the neck. But then I realized that the great snipe in question was standing with its beak open, and it wasn't a double beak, it was the upper bill and the lower bill of the same beak. There were also giant snipes and imperial snipes. Imperial snipes! And the jack snipe, which was smaller and had "shorter legs" than the common snipe, according to the *Great Norwegian Encyclopedia*. But the best thing about the jack snipe, apart from its name, I thought, was that it sounded like a galloping horse when it plummeted through the air. I could just imagine it: that I was standing on a heath and could hear a horse galloping toward me, then I turned to face the sound and instead saw a falling bird. I started to cry again. That was me. I was standing on the heath listening to what I'd once been, but then I saw myself approaching. Not a galloping horse, but a falling bird.

My supervisor called me one day when I was walking in the mountains alone. I saw her name run across the screen again and again, but couldn't bring myself to answer. What was I going to say? That I'd had my period and everything I knew about birds had been sucked out of me along with it? Yes, I know, it's unbelievable. Yes, it really is a shame. Yes,

I'm reading for dear life now. I know the differences among
a common snipe, a great snipe, and a jack snipe. I reached
the tarn that I'd set as my destination. The surface was still,
and there, on a small stone out in the water, I spotted what
I believed was a common snipe, incredibly enough. He was
standing on one leg, motionless, and looked like he was wading, as we say about birds who watch the surface of the water
for food. Because I couldn't stop myself in time when I saw
him, he heard me and flew up. And it was then that I could
confirm that it was a common snipe and not a great snipe.
Because, unlike the great snipe, the common snipe does not
fly straight up, but zigzags here and there, just as this example of the snipe family had done. Yes, I said to myself, as
though I'd just won a competition. But there was not so much
as a ripple on the water, the mountains remained silent and
orange, majestic with white peaks, the October day was cold
and clear, and there was no one else here to witness that I'd
managed to guess right, it meant nothing to my surroundings. Was that why I felt so sad? I suddenly pictured Hans's
little frightened face in the doorway, when he thought that
I wanted him to identify the tit I was holding in my hand,
whereas in fact I just wanted to know what on earth it was.
What had I become, I thought as I sat there on a stone by the
water and peeled an orange, someone who got angry with
their kids when they couldn't classify a tit? I took a deep

breath. What was it I was feeling, why did I suddenly want to cry, why did it feel like my heart was broken, the kind of grief you feel when something you have lost still exists? The water gave no answer, nor did the mountains, but the air around me was sparklingly clear.

THE THREAD

There is no one else in the pool. The surface of the water is shiny and still, and the water is deep and light blue. No one knows that I'm slipping into the water now.

But it seems that I'm dreaming.

I see my hand down there on the duvet, thin and wrinkled. I'm not in a pool at all. I'm in my room in the care home, and it's eight o'clock in the morning. It's St. Lucia's Day, the festival of light in midwinter, and I'm waiting for someone to come in and sing for me. I just fell asleep while I was waiting. I'm waiting to hear someone singing in the distance, down the corridor, and to hear them come closer and closer, like a small river . . . Dark the night falls, hiding stables and homes . . . When I was little, this was the day I longed for when December came around. It was the dark, and the tinsel, and the light, and the Lucia song that made everything glittery, secret, and safe. Here in my room, it's pitch-black. Well: the emergency exit sign above the door is lit. There's also some light outside the window, it must be from the small park just opposite. Light enough for me to see the tube that rises up like a silent whisper from my hand to the shiny bag on the stand beside me. I didn't think I'd experience this feeling again, that I'm so happy that I feel I have to run, but it's actually running through me now, as I lie here and will never run again. The Lucia procession will come and sing for me. They will come in with burning candles. As I imagine I will do too, soon. My light is running out into the dark like a small river.

Can I be in a care home and not in a hospital, if I have a drip in my hand? And who am "I," in fact, in this short story? It can't possibly be me, me with my hand on the duvet. I can't possibly be in a short story, and it can't be me who's the narrator. And yet . . . It's as if that which could have been me is gathered in the single word *I* and allows all these possibilities to play out at the same time, in the present, as these sentences claim it's happening now, here. If it were actually true that I was now lying in a room in a care home or hospital and dozing in and out of this moment, I wouldn't be able to communicate it to anyone, to you, like this. But it seems I'm able to do it, all the same, and it puzzles me. It's possible that I am a character in a movie. I imagine that the correct way for my condition to be communicated would not be through a thread of thoughts and words, but rather images, which would slide slowly past your eyes. Images of the pool. Images of my hand. Images of my daughter. A slow motion of the drip moving up toward the ceiling, illuminated by the soft light from the park outside. My daughter slipped in there suddenly, unintroduced, but that's because she's something I'm thinking about, something that lies behind all the other stuff that has surfaced in me, like things rise to the surface in a bog. I'm thinking that when it happens, when my light runs out into the dark like a small river, I want my daughter to be with me. She will sit by my bedside and see my light flowing out. My daughter, Gunnhild, who lives in Denmark.

In many ways it's quite strange, I have to say, that she lives in Denmark, because when she was a child, Gunnhild was always so upset that she had the same name as the wicked Queen Gunnhild who lived in the tenth century. If I was going to have a queen's name, could it not have been a *good* queen instead! she said to me, angrily. And not a queen that was found in a bog hundreds of years later! Queen Gunnhild was lured to Denmark after her husband died, I'm sure you remember. She was going to marry Harald Bluetooth, but what Harald Bluetooth did was lure her there, then drown her in a bog. And when the villagers found a body in the bog at Vejle in the 1800s, they believed it was Queen Gunnhild who had risen again. Aha, that must have been the thought underlying all the other thoughts rising up in me, when I thought that the way in which I was communicating these thoughts of mine, rising up in me, was like things slowly rising up in a bog. It was this body in the bog all the time. Anyway, they later found out that it wasn't the wicked Queen Gunnhild who had been found in the bog, it turned out it was an ordinary woman, pinned down in the bog by wooden pegs at the elbows and knees.

Now I want the Lucia procession to come soon and sing for me, and give me something to drink. But there's not a sound in the corridor. Not even a Lucia bun falling from the piled-high basket and hitting the linoleum with a dull bun thud. I want them to phone Gunnhild and tell her she has to come quickly. That she must drop whatever she has in her hands and come.

What does make me happy, though, is to think that these thoughts of mine have been communicated to you, even though I'm lying here without being able to move much at all, because they have. I have no idea how, I barely know that I thought them. And yet they have risen up here in this room, almost weightless, I feel that I can see them, I feel that I can see my thoughts, they're floating just under the ceiling, flickering past; my hand, the pool, the bog, Queen Gunnhild, my daughter. Now I'm communicating to you the image of my own thin, wrinkled hand trying to grasp something in the air, but it catches nothing and falls back to rest on the white duvet. I wonder if it's you that I'm trying to grasp, as though you were the end of a thread.

THE THREAD 2

Protest

We herewith wish to submit a written complaint against the previous text. We wish to protest that it ends with the old lady lying there, thirsty, waiting and fumbling for something ungraspable in the air in a room, and that no one comes. If one watches a nature program and sees unbearable situations—that is different. One then often sees terrible things, but without the expectation that someone will intervene and change the sequence of events. Like when one sees polar bear cubs starving to death, or when one sees orcas killing seals, or when one sees lions running and jumping up on an elephant and biting the elephant's neck and after a long time forcing the bleeding and exhausted elephant to its knees. In such cases, one cannot expect that the person filming will intervene, even though one might hope they would when one is a child. As an adult, one does not expect it, one knows that wildlife photographers cannot change the course of nature, or a predator's nature, or put themselves in danger in order to distract a hungry lion. But in fiction: here every possibility is available. We wish to point this out here in protest, and also to point out that it should not be necessary to have to point this out at all. One does not have to let an old woman lie alone, confused and half dreaming, longing for her daughter in Denmark, in a hospital room or a care home room with an emergency exit sign shining green above the door. And on St. Lucia's Day, of all days.

We would like to propose that you expand the previous text. We propose that the woman can be lying in bed, as she is, but then suddenly she hears someone at the door. This makes her happy, because she thinks it's one of the care workers. She's particularly fond of a care worker called Torunn, she hopes that it's Torunn. But it's not Torunn, because Torunn is at the dentist's—in comes a lion instead. The lion moves slowly toward the bed and the old woman, who should also have a name, we suggest Nikka, as it sounds old. It would be good if Nikka tries to lift her head a little at this point, to see if she can see Torunn, but sees that it can't be Torunn after all, as the unexpected visitor is far too short. The lion will now, at our suggestion, approach the bed. In a nature program, the lion would jump up onto Nikka and bite her with the intention of eating her, and the lion would stand on Nikka and eat her up until no one could say for sure, before doing a dental exam on what remained of Nikka's teeth, that it was in fact Nikka who had been lying there—and it was. But: because this is fiction, things don't need to take the same course that they would in a nature program. The photographer, who in this case is you, the author, can instead write that the lion goes over to the small table, where an enormous pork chop has been left untouched because Nikka is far too old and her teeth are too bad for her to be able to chew it. The lion can now grab the chop in her mouth (because it has to be reasonable that the lion doesn't eat Nikka, even though she has the chance) and trot happily out.

Sudden interventions like this can happen. Do you recall that on February 7, 1910, Virginia Woolf dressed up as an Abyssinian prince and boarded the jewel in the crown of the Royal Navy, HMS *Dreadnought*, together with five friends from the Bloomsbury Group? It's known as "the *Dreadnought* hoax" and the Royal Navy was horrified that it had truly believed it was being visited by six princes, who in fact were only six authors, who they treated royally for real. Well, we've always liked to imagine how quiet it must have been in the boat as they approached the ship, the six, and to think about Virginia's plan to keep her mouth shut, as she would give away that she was a woman if she said anything, and that she succeeded in her plan. If we close our eyes, we can imagine the sound of the sea in the dark against the prow of the boat, where the six were sitting in disguise. The gentle clucking. The even oar strokes, the "princes" rowing steadily toward the ship. The fact that we can do this, almost *be* at the prow of the boat of the prince pretenders, is evidence enough, we believe, to condemn the previous text: our ability to imagine would have no problem picking up the phone to ring Gunnhild in Denmark, and Gunnhild would be able to come, problem solved, and we would then not have to think that there are old people hovering between wakefulness and half death, with an emergency exit light shining far too symbolically above the door—that they exist, and that these half states exist too, without any obvious or lightning-flash solution.

THE THREAD 3

Small letter from Queen Gunnhild

In the small letter we found under the door (it's perhaps more of a note, pushed in through the gap between the door and the doorframe), it says that Queen Gunnhild is unfortunately unable to come. She is, at the time of writing, transformed into a swallow and sitting outside a loft window in Scotland, screeching and screeching so that Egil Skallagrimsson cannot concentrate on composing the poem of praise he is sitting inside the loft trying to write, which he wants to present to Eric Bloodaxe, Queen Gunnhild's husband, who intends to chop off Egil's head tomorrow. You can read about this, Queen Gunnhild writes, in *Egil's Saga*, where it explains in note no. 124 that a "shape-shifter" is someone who can change shape with the help of magic, and then says "it must have been Gunnhild who has transformed herself into a swallow," and she just wants to confirm that that is the case, so there is no doubt whatsoever. We stand in this breeze from the past, fluttering. Queen Gunnhild. Screeching swallow. Shape-shifter. Slowly we come to ourselves again and go out onto the veranda to breathe in some fresh air. The sun is going down over the fjord, a tourist boat lies peacefully on the water, present time—did the present twitch at this unexpected letter, or did it stand as solid as cast concrete? A magpie lands on the ridge of a roof, we eye it skeptically, but it seems there can be little doubt that it is just a magpie, and not the evil Queen Gunnhild, who did her best to annoy the author in the loft so he could not write a single verse.

THE THREAD 4

The lion comments

I didn't know quite what to think when I felt something tug at my tail. As far as I knew, I was completely alone in the room, and there were no elephants nearby, no long trunks, or other lions that might nibble my tail to tease me. I turned around and saw what it was: a wrinkled old hand that was pulling my tail as though it were the end of a thread. I was on my way over to a chop that was lying on a table, as far as I can remember, but then suddenly felt my whole body shudder—the grip of the wrinkled old hand was the reason. I saw no arm attached to the hand, nothing other than a sudden hand that appeared out of nowhere at the end of my tail. Of course it frightened me, I admit. It felt like I was in the middle of my worst nightmare: that something that isn't there suddenly intervenes and prevents me from reaching a pork chop. But then the hand disappeared, back to where it came from, I suppose. Could one expect that an intervention such as this, from nowhere, voiceless and terrifying, would change nothing about the way one lived? That one could still totally trust one's surroundings and not watch one's tail at all times and tuck it under oneself when one sleeps? No. But, and I say this with absolute conviction: if someone pulls your tail because they clearly think you're a thread, know that the connection you offer in standing there, albeit unwillingly and only for a few seconds, was perhaps enough for whoever needed a thread to pull—that those hands understood that they weren't just fumbling in a big and empty room without ever finding something to hold. They found you, you were there, and they could sigh with relief: ah yes, not alone after all.

EVIL FLOWERS

"No one thought these flowers could actually harm anyone, but they could!" said Vendel in a loud, clear voice. She was sitting, as always, on the first seat to the right, which meant she had direct access to me, and if that seat was taken, she would sit on the seat behind me, lean forward, and talk into the back of my head. I looked up in the mirror and saw that she was reading from a piece of paper. "They stood there in the garden, so small and beautiful," Vendel read, "in lots of different colors, which made you want to pick them and put them together in a bunch, but God help anyone who picked them, because then something awful and unexpected would happen." I hoped she would soon be done. I didn't want to hear any more, I wanted to drive my bus in peace. "For example," Vendel said, "the person who picks the flowers might trip on their way up the stairs with the flowers in their hand as if someone had pushed them, or they might get scalded by hot water from the tap, they might burn the porridge, deeply offend a neighbor, suffer a huge loss on the stock exchange, slip in the shower, or, in the worst case, be run over and killed one warm summer's day." I stopped the bus to let on an old man and a teenager. Vendel kept quiet while the man paid his fare. As soon as I had closed the doors and the man had tottered past us, she started again. "These flowers," Vendel read, "were quite simply malicious and evil, and no one in their right mind should have them in their garden. If anyone should take it upon themselves to rid the world of all evil, they should start with these flowers. Look out for the small white labels, the kind you find when you buy plants in the shop, you know, the ones that are stuck in the pot with information about light conditions and planting depth and when they flower and things like that, and see if it says 'evil flowers.' Because they're the ones, and you can safely get rid of them." She almost shouted the last sentence, before bellowing with laughter: "Well, safely, maybe not!"

I gave her a short haha, the kind of haha that the evil stepmother in "Cinderella" laughs when she pictures Cinderella going to the ball. I was so tired of Vendel. I had stopped driving taxis because I was tired of the customers, I was tired of all their chat. I was perhaps a bit different from my old taxi colleagues, because most of them were real chatterboxes. But not me. I just liked driving cars. When I was a taxi driver, my boss told me in an appraisal that the others found it unnerving that I never spoke to them and just sat in my car when we were at a stand in the center of town, that I seemed to keep myself to myself. I'd apparently driven home some friends of one of the other drivers, and they'd told their friend that they'd never had such an unpleasant driver, they'd felt that I would rather not have anyone in my taxi, that I'd just stared grimly at the road ahead when they asked even ordinary questions, or given monosyllabic answers. I didn't try to change, I just stopped driving taxis and started on the buses instead. Because here, no one should distract the driver, that's what it says on the sign by the door. DO NOT DISTURB THE DRIVER. But Vendel could certainly do just that. To begin with, I suspected that she took the bus solely so she could talk, because she only ever rode the entire route, as far as her ticket would take her, and never got off before she was back at her stop, but this was no longer a suspicion—now I knew. She took the bus to talk. I had tried to change to the night shift, but that didn't help, there she was at her bus stop at 7:18 p.m., where previously she had stood at 11:18 a.m., ready and waiting. Had she hacked the bus company system to find out when I was at work? But the others said the same. Vendel, yes, they said, when I decided to share my problem in the staff room one day. We know her. Is she talking you into the ground? they said, and I nodded. I could cope with everything, I could cope with screaming children, angry drug addicts, too much hair spray, feet on the seats, boisterous school classes, I could cope with them all, but I could not cope with Vendel. I felt her lean toward me, she was repeating and repeating something. Huh? I said. What do *you* think? Vendel said. Do you think it was good? What? I said. The text! Vendel said. I don't know, I said, I'm driving the bus, I have to concentrate.

Here I unfortunately have to stop the story abruptly, without any explanation other than that what I've told thus far is not true. I'm not a bus driver, I was never a taxi driver before becoming a bus driver, and I'm not fed up with Vendel, who doesn't exist. In other words, it's all made up. If we had been going through a forest, we would now have arrived at a clearing: the truth. Had it been a dream, we would be at that difficult point when someone shakes you and you wake up. Had it been a photograph that one had put in developer and watched as the image slowly but surely appeared on the paper, I would have to say that what *did* happen today, if I was going to stick to the facts in the clear developer, was that at the gym I was followed, not by an irritating passenger, but by an obnoxious older man who wanted to joke around and be silly on every single machine that I used. It started when we were side by side on the rowing machines. It's an incredibly small gym, the one that I'm talking about, down in a basement, and I suspect the owners have squeezed in all the equipment (which they must have bought from another gym that was going to be redone, because it's all very old and creaky and there are missing cushions and padding and the like) as closely as possible in order to make as much money as possible, so they have only three rowing machines, which are as close together as they can be without those training on them bumping into each other when they lean back with their elbows well out to each side. Anyway, he sat next to me, he didn't choose the third rowing machine, which is on the outside, he chose the one in the middle, so that he would be as close as possible, and then he sat there joking about rowing and fishing until I cut short my warm-up and answered as politely as I could, before I went over to the leg machine. He followed me there, and chose the machine beside me and joked about how he was now trying to get rid of his belly. So I went over to the extremely minimal mat training area, where we all have to position ourselves as best we can in relation to each other on the mats, which are actually more like dishcloths, just big enough to make us feel that we're not rolling around on the dirty floor. And he followed me there, too, and did sit-ups while he carried on joking about his belly. Eventually, I walked away from him and lay down right next to the wall bars, the tiniest space for mat work that I've ever seen, with enough room for only one person who can then use the mat, the wall bars, or the only sling in the gym, and what did he do but come over and start using the sling, which was attached in such a way that

he could lean half over me on the floor as he joked about his
arm muscles.

But while Vendel and my own identity as a taciturn and jaded
bus driver are made up, the flowers are not made up. They
are in fact true, even though I have written a text about them.
The nature of the truth about something does not change
simply because it exists in a text, even though I have demon-
strated the opposite in the case of Vendel. The flowers are
frightening, and I know that things have been written about
evil flowers in literature before, we all know that Charles
Baudelaire, the French poet, wrote the collection *Les Fleurs
du mal*, which was published in 1857 in France, and is called
The Flowers of Evil in English (personally, I think a better title
would be *Evil's Flowers* or *The Flowers from Hell*, or, worst-case
scenario, my own title, *Evil Flowers*), but his flowers are a
metaphor. Here, in this text, they are very real. And they are
therefore also true. I stand by everything I've said about the
flowers, except, of course, that they were written by a certain
"Vendel."

What happened in my case, after I had picked a bunch of
what proved to be evil flowers, was that I broke two small
bones on the underside of my foot. I couldn't walk for three
months. After much googling, I found out there was a doctor

in Oslo who could operate on these painful small bones, and I had the right foot operated on, but didn't dare operate on the left. And it was there on the operating table that I started to think about the bunch of flowers I had picked on the day that I felt the pain under my foot, and I realized that I had been unlucky enough to pick evil flowers. They were growing by the edge of the road, hidden in among normal roadside flowers, red clover, red campion, purple geranium, and buttercups. And they blazed in unusual colors, neon white, turquoise, hot pink, and neon yellow. So I took the ones I'd never seen before. The bunch was unbelievably beautiful. But I hadn't, I realized on the operating table, taken many steps with the bunch in my hand before I felt a sharp pain under both my feet. Oh no, evil flowers, I whispered to myself as I lay there staring at a cabinet that had glass panels, which meant that, if I wanted to, I could watch the reflection of the operation in the glass and see how the surgeon hacked away at the sesamoid bone to detach it from the rest of my skeleton, he hacked away for a whole hour before he could show it to me, big and bloody like a tooth. He had come home from Miami the night before, and the sweat trickled out from under his green scrub hat and ran down his sunburned skin.

Because of this problem with my feet, I have to wear sneakers both inside and out, and I spend a lot of time worrying about the sneakers I have, which work, that they will go out of production, and what, in that case, will replace them. Experience has shown that they're always replaced by something unusable. I've often bought five pairs of the same shoes when I finally find some that don't hurt, but somehow I don't dare to buy ten, and I can't afford to either. I even have shoe-focused nightmares, which often end with the shoes being ruined, or with me having to walk without any shoes at all. The last one took place in an endlessly long train station in San Francisco, and it was raining, indoors as well, so my white sneakers turned brown and were ruined, by what I understood in a kind of dream perspective was a small round turd inside the shoe. Was it anxiety, plain and simple? In the form of a small round turd? Then there was something about a woman lying in a bed in a long, narrow room shouting that she was waiting for a surgeon, she waved, and I wanted to rush out, because I understood that this was turning into a shoe nightmare, and then I discovered that I had taken my shoe off and I was caught.

In closing, I would like to say that I wonder what Baudelaire would have said if he'd discovered that his title had been used in a short story about the problems of sesamoid bones and sneakers going out of production, and obnoxious people in gyms and made-up bus drivers and passengers. I think he would have pursed his lips. I think he would have had his thin hair combed over to one side. I think he would have had a large silk cravat around his neck, and been surrounded by darkness. I think he would have glared angrily at the camera, so angrily that he looked frightening. In fact, I think that what he was thinking in the author portrait from 1863—having just had a glimpse of the future and this very text—was *Evil flowers, my ass.*

A BIT LIKE THIS

PROTEST

We would like to protest that the photograph has been printed *without the photographer, Étienne Carjat, being credited.* We protest that not even a word is said about Baudelaire being highly critical of the art of photography, and that it is perhaps *this* that we see piercing through his gaze aimed at the poor photographer, and *not* the highly unlikely possibility that Baudelaire had caught a glimpse of the future and read the "Evil Flowers" story in this very collection and so was angry and upset about it just as Carjat pressed the shutter button on his camera. Nor do we hear a word about the possibility that this tetchiness might also reveal an anger toward himself. After all, he must, as he allowed himself to be photographed in the first place, have had a wish to be eternalized, and thus not to disappear into oblivion, even though it went against his intellectual and artistic convictions. His angry, self-loathing gaze will now pierce the universe forever.

We also protest that the photograph stands alone without
any text, only a title that says "A Bit Like This." This makes
"the text" (which is not even there! A photograph is all there
is!) too open, it can be interpreted in any possible way. We
suggest that Baudelaire would be better placed in some con-
text or other. If you've read the American writer Richard
Brautigan's small cycle of nine poems about Baudelaire, you
will have seen how this can be done. Baudelaire gets up to all
kinds of things. He drives a Model A, he is followed by an in-
sane asylum all over California, he even helps to grind coffee,
and he assists with bird funerals, where, for example, he re-
cites prayers "the size of / dead birds." It will become apparent
to you just how much can be done with dramatization. For
example, as inspiration: we were once accused of not being
in touch with our own feelings. Here we notice that it's hard
to continue from the perspective of the royal *we*. Because
it wasn't the case that the man was in love with the entire
analysis department. No, there was a man who, to my great
consternation, was in love with me. And I didn't realize, I
had tried to be as friendly as I could, even though something
about the man made me feel uneasy; to be frank, I thought
he was a fool. I really had to make an effort to be nice so he
wouldn't notice how I felt deep down. It was, for me, this
strained effort that must have been misconstrued as flirting,
and it always makes me sad for women and men when I think
about it. In fact, I felt something akin to scorn for the man,

who was a colleague in the analysis department, by the way, and who thought he was smarter than me, and that he produced better analyses. I'll soon get to the point. But just listen to this risible analysis: One Friday when we were out having payday beers, he told me that he'd been in love with me for a long time, but that now he was over it. His reasoning was as follows: he had noticed that I kept my distance from him, which he took to mean that I was "afraid to let myself go" as I was not ready for "the strong, turbulent feelings," that I was "unable to plumb the depths of my own emotions." These were all qualities he looked for in a person, and as I did not have these qualities, his own feelings had cooled, and he was no longer in love with me. He just wanted to tell me that. I couldn't help but laugh in shock, internally of course, as I had no such emotions to plumb, for him, unless they were the very opposite of those he was talking about, and I said, Well, that's a shame, and that was the end of the conversation, for my part.

Every time I saw the portrait of Baudelaire, I had to think of him, his unbending darkness, I imagined that he looked exactly like Baudelaire's face here, when he realized that I was unable to plumb the depths of my own emotions, and that I, contrary to what he had thought, was therefore weak and not strong. But often I see just Baudelaire in the photograph, and those are the best times. Oh, how many times have I stared

into the portrait of Baudelaire and tried to understand what
it is that he's staring at, until it feels like we're staring at the
quivering marrow at the core of existence, and as soon as it
appears, this marrow feels incomprehensible, as though what
we've actually been doing is repeating in fierce competition,
marrow, until the word loses all meaning and could mean
anything from fish cake to hubcap to sorrow, and Baudelaire's
eyes slip slowly backward and into his head again and close
on the page in front of me.

But now this protest has turned *completely* into anecdote and
we can only apologize profusely. And there you see the pits
and hollows that lie in wait for you the moment you abandon
the royal *we*!

ESCAPE

One morning, completely out of the blue, Ruth suggested that we stop the whole cell pistol thing. We were sitting eating breakfast, each with a cell pistol by our plate, but Ruth's was slightly closer to the edge of the table than mine. I noticed it when we sat down, it was a small detail that made me uneasy—the cell pistol should be closer to the plate. Do you mean just us or society as a whole? I asked as I buttered my toast. I mean the two of us and society as a whole. Everyone. She gave me an audacious look as she pushed her cell pistol even closer to the edge of the table. Hm, I said, to keep from letting on that it made me nervous that she was pushing her cell pistol away. I think we should all hand our cell pistols in. Children shouldn't be given a cell pistol for their tenth birthday anymore. I think we should separate the pistol and the telephone functions, like before. Just as she said that, the grip of my cell pistol flashed blue. It was a reminder: Write foreword for "Photograph of the Year" catalog, it said. Interesting thought, I said, but I think society is well organized and safe. I took my cell pistol in one hand and my plate in the other, put the plate down on the kitchen counter, tidied away the jam and cheese that I knew Ruth wouldn't use, and said that I had to go up to the office. She sat and looked out the window with a pensive expression on her face, and I saw her push her cell pistol even farther away, right over to the other side of the table, without looking at it, before she leaned back in her chair and continued to look out of the window, as though she was practicing a life without cell pistols.

Up in the office, I tried to write the foreword. Of all the photographs I had seen that year, one in particular, of a small cat in China, had stayed with me. The photograph was taken in a park, there were people sitting on benches next to a green iron railing, and behind the railing there was some beautiful tall ornamental grass. If one focused only on the right side of the picture, which covered half the frame, one saw people talking to each other, people walking and looking at their cell pistols, a mother with a child on a tricycle—in short, an ordinary day in the park. One might think that it was simply a very good and lively picture of a park. But then one would notice that to the left of the railing, out in the tall grass, was a small cat. The cat's head was stretched up with obvious interest. The clear blue eyes were looking at something out

of the frame, beyond all the people. One could not see what
it was looking at, but could see that it was very interested. A
bird, perhaps?

But before I go on, I must tell you about my relationship to
ornamental grass. If one thinks about the many things one
can have a relationship to in this life, ornamental grass is
definitely one of them. Sooner or later, a person will encoun-
ter ornamental grass. For example, when one is a child, and
someone in the immediate family plants ornamental grass
in the garden, something that one, as a child, could not
understand, because it's ugly, and boring, and a nuisance,
because if one is playing bocce in the garden and is unlucky
enough that one of the green, yellow, or red balls rolls too
far, it can disappear into the long ornamental grass and one
will have to look for it there. It's horrible, the grass is cold
and sharp and scratches your bare child arms as you search
for the ball. Ornamental grass is worse than hosta, a plant
that many people fell in love with in the early eighties. The
hosta has big, boring leaves with white variegation, which
stand and scream *Disgusting, disgusting* in the garden; some
might say that I was an aesthetically oversensitive child to
have reacted to something as ordinary as ornamental grass
and hosta, but when I reflect on it now, it's possible that I
reacted precisely because they were so ordinary. But I didn't
like bleeding hearts either, even though the flowers are pink

and heart-shaped and hang from the stem. The only flowers
I really loved were snowflakes and lilies of the valley. And
they were, truth be told, less often seen than ornamental
grass and hosta. If one thinks about the difference between
lilies of the valley and ornamental grass, it's perhaps quite
obvious why I thought ornamental grass was so awful; it's because lily of the valley has such beautifully shaped bells that
smell so sweet, whereas the only visual form the grass has to
offer is a gentle curve. If one is fortunate enough to stumble
upon a belt of flowering lilies of the valley in the forest just
as the sunlight filters through the trees and touches the forest
floor and the green leaves and the small white bells so everything is luminous, one might experience the same quiet but
effervescent joy that one feels when one understands that the
person one loves loves one back, and if one imagines sunlight on ornamental grass in the same way, one will perhaps
see that sunlight on ornamental grass isn't anything more
than what it is: sunlight, ornamental grass. And yet I now
have large terra-cotta pots in what I call my garden, which is
nothing more than a concrete square outside the house, with
tall ornamental grass in them. Why? Because as an adult I
love things other than small, perfumed bells. I love it when
the wind blows through the grass, it reminds me of sand
and being by the sea. And it was actually me, not Ruth, who
suggested that we fill the pots with ornamental grass. It was

a strange day in my life, and I can still hear myself saying: What about ornamental grass? As long as you pay for it, Ruth said.

So I was sitting in the office trying to write the foreword to the "Photograph of the Year" catalog and thinking about the photograph of the cat in the ornamental grass in China, when I looked up and out the window and saw that where usually there are tall pine trees on the other side of the road, there was now tall ornamental grass, and in the middle of the ornamental grass a small cat face with light blue eyes was staring up at me attentively. I looked down at the desktop to somehow clear my eyes so I could look up again, focus, and see pine trees and the usual view, but the usual view was not there, all I saw was ornamental grass and a cat with light blue eyes. In the photograph I was going to write about, the cat was sitting in profile, but here the cat was looking at me head-on—and after the instant when I realized it was looking straight at me, which might possibly mean that it was me the cat in the photograph was looking at with such interest the whole time, that I was thus *in* the photograph I was going to write about, everything became too confused for me to tell it in a way that would be coherent: Is it true that Ruth came screaming up the stairs with ornamental grass growing around her? Is it true that I opened the window and shot the cat so blood leaped out of its head and its two light blue eyes bounced to each side like marbles? Is it true that I only meant to take a photograph of it and for the first time pressed the wrong button, something the designers of the cell pistol said was impossible, that the inbuilt intelligence in a cell pistol would understand that one was pressing the wrong button and thus not fire any shots? Is it true that the ornamental grass stopped growing around Ruth at that moment, and that Ruth stopped screaming, in shock? I don't know, everything in my head is a such mess from the moment I realized the cat was sitting with its head facing me, but what is true is that I wrote a piece for the newspaper about what had happened, that there was a furor, that the cell pistol manufacturer halted all production of the new cell pistol until it had found the error, and as a result the cell pistol became history, as did I, you'll find me on Wikipedia if you search for "cell pistol." But that isn't really what interests me. What interests me here is the ornamental grass, and the fact that Ruth one morning pushed her cell pistol away from its usual place by her plate, and that she leaned back in her chair with her arms crossed after she had pushed it even farther away, which it doesn't say on Wikipedia; it seems to be the kind of everyday detail that will always escape.

THE CLIFFS, WHEN DEAD

To get to the top of the White Cliffs of Dover was not that hard. It was, in principle, just a matter of walking. Moving one foot in front of the other, up a narrow, romantic path through the green grass. The hardest part was getting to England in the first place. Being a neurotic and booking flights could be problematic. Veronika knew all about that. Because she was a neurotic.

She was also dead.

And it was difficult for dead people to book flights to England, or anywhere else in the world, for that matter. Being a neurotic and dead when trying to buy a plane ticket was a combination that not many before her had tried. But someone had to be the first! said Veronika to encourage herself as she sat there and typed in her date of birth on the carrier's website, but she could not find anywhere to give her date of death.

For really, what did she feel, come back after all these years and Mrs.
Ramsay dead? Nothing, nothing—nothing that she could express at
all, mumbled the dead Veronika, on the plane bound for England, quietly, so no one would hear her. Various quotes from
Virginia Woolf's *To the Lighthouse*, on which Veronika had written a thesis when she was still alive, tended to pop up in Veronika's head—even now, in the afterlife. Did she feel nothing?
Nothing she could express at all? No! She felt excited that she
was going to see the White Cliffs, which she had always been
drawn to, without ever quite understanding why. Were they
alluring because they were so white, because they resembled
an enormous marshmallow that had been cut with a spoon,
because they revealed something extremely white that somehow was there in the depths of existence, and, if one thinks
about what chalk is made from, i.e., fossilized remains, in fact
they resembled a kind of geological skeleton? Was it the shape,
was it the color, was it that they stood there, so weather-beaten
and white, alone against the sea? It's not always easy to explain why one is drawn to something! But in Veronika's mind,
when she, to her surprise, woke up from the great nothingness
of the dead, and was a ghost with flesh, a person in a dead
format, a kind of living version, there was only one thought:
that she now had the chance to get to the White Cliffs of Dover.

What was it like to lie dead in the earth? Veronika thought
about it as she sat on the airplane, looking through the

in-flight magazine—that being dead was a bit like the light outside on a January afternoon when the sun has set and the snow on the ground that barely covers the moss (which sticks up here and there) creates a thin white light across the pale blue sky, and between the slender, leafless birch trees on the mound, but enough for everything to look eerie and transparent, if one looks close enough. The usual view through the window looks, in this light, extraordinary. And yet ordinary. That was what it was like being dead. Just BOOM: strange, but normal light.

And if she were to choose the episode from her life that would best illustrate what it was like to be alive, she thought, as she followed the narrow path through the grass up toward the cliffs, it would have to be the time she was going to meet the head of the Danish analysis department for the first time, and stood outside the hotel and the representative from the Dutch analysis department was standing there as well, waiting, a woman twenty years younger than herself. They were both wearing dresses in the same color, mustard yellow. And they had the same white stripes on their dresses. But Veronika's also had polka dots. I've also got polka dots, Veronika said, joking. The young woman laughed politely. That's what it was like to be alive. It was to have the same dress, but not quite the same, and to point it out because you felt it was necessary, because it was so obvious, and to elicit polite laughter,

which said: You didn't need to point that out, because it's
so obvious, it would have been more dignified not to. To be
alive was to not know what dignified behavior was. And now,
well, it was too late to acquire more knowledge about what
counted as dignified behavior. Now she was dead, and finally
on her way up toward the cliffs of Dover. Veronika, the dead
neurotic. It was, she felt with great intensity, incredible that
she was here. More incredible than the fact that she was dead.
The cliffs really were so white, they were actually as white
as her skin, whiter than chalk, whiter than anything alive,
white like layer upon layer of death. So this was how it was
to experience the cliffs when dead. Suddenly to understand
the obvious parallel. As though what she had always been
drawn to, without knowing it, was an aspect of herself—her
future state in death. The cliffs stood there, as white as before
and just as unaware that a dead person was walking toward
them, a person who had dreamed of seeing them all her life,
and had finally succeeded, when dead.

They were: as unseeing over the water, as unfeeling and un-
thinking as the White Cliffs of Dover had always been.

WHITE DOVE BECOMES BLACK CROW

It was a very ordinary Sunday. The light was gentle and Sunday-like on the hedges of the residential area. Residential areas on Sunday, and hedges in particular, are stressful, I've always thought, so I was glad when I could finally get out to the old road that runs along the fjord. There were seldom any cars here after a tunnel for the new highway had been blasted through the mountain behind the residential area, and it was a nice place to walk. Nothing had been unordinary at all until now, then suddenly, there, in the middle of the road, was a white dove. She was sitting so still that I wondered if she might be made of plaster, if she was a kind of garden gnome in the form of a dove that one of the gangs of youths cruising in their old Volvos had stolen from a garden and left in the middle of the road. Yes, that was my first thought: I blamed the youths who obeyed no one, and who were constantly being written about in the local papers, and who I could hear at night when I was trying to sleep, streaks of throbbing engines through the center, out along the fjord. But now I saw that her feathers were fluttering, that the dove was looking at me, her head tilted slightly in my direction as though she was listening to something. And then the following happened: From the top of her dove head to the tip of her dove tail, the bird changed color. The dove slowly but surely slipped into black, millimeter by millimeter, until there could be no doubt that it was a black crow standing in front of me, on the very same spot. The same slight ruffling in the plumage. The same listening expression in what we would have to call the face, as though she were leaning in my direction. And then the crow took flight, and I heard her say—apologies, but what on earth is the verb for the noise that crows make: *to crow*?— a few hoarse *caw caw*s as she flew into the forest, which, I have forgotten to say, flanks the road on both sides.

I had been so astonished that I'd forgotten to film it. No one would believe it, I scarcely believed it myself. But I had seen it! I had, in practice, seen a miracle, I, who had always dreamed of seeing a miracle, had now seen a miracle. As a child, it was the stories of biblical miracles that grabbed me, for example, that Jesus walked on water, or that Moses divided the sea and walked through it without getting wet feet. I could picture it so vividly, so clearly, how the water divided and rose up into two light blue, transparent walls where stunned fish swam happily along, then unexpectedly bumped into the invisible barrier. However, after many years of living in the material world, I had learned that miracles did not exist, other than in stories. Normal just repeated itself ad infinitum. But now: I had seen a white dove shape-shift into a black crow, I was standing barely a meter from them, it, and it had happened. Should I call the local newspaper? I thought about the story I had just read, about the man who had been hiking in the mountains and stumbled upon what he believed to be part of a dinosaur tooth, but which, once it had been analyzed, turned out to be a piece of goat's horn, and decided not to. After all, I had nothing to support my claim, and I could see the picture of myself under the headline WHITE DOVE BECOMES BLACK CROW, I was smiling sheepishly at the camera and the text let on that the journalist had done the interview only because the paper didn't have enough material for the Friday edition.

It was also worth noting, I thought, when I finally walked past the point of transformation with some trepidation (because what if I was transformed myself? It didn't happen) and then on into the woods along the old highway, that even if one was going to witness a transformation, this was a rather boring and stupid transformation. WHITE dove. BLACK crow. If there was going to be a transformation from one thing to another, why could it not be two completely

different things? Why could it not have been WHITE DOVE
BECOMES BIG ELK. Or WHITE DOVE BECOMES GREEN
TOOTHBRUSH. Or WHITE DOVE BECOMES WHITE
CHEESE. The historical symbolism that these two birds, the
dove and the crow, had been recognized as carrying was also
a little boring. The dove as a symbol of peace, the crow as . . .
had I confused it with the raven here? The raven was often
seen to be a bad omen. The only famous crows I could think
of were Hugin and Munin, they were Odin's crows, carriers
of knowledge. Or were they ravens? In which case, didn't
they represent insight rather than misfortune? I had to get
home to my books, to check if Ovid had any metamorphoses
that were as elementary as this. Then I heard the crow sound
again, I looked up, and because I did it so quickly, I managed to step over the edge of the asphalt and twist my ankle.
It was so painful I felt sick. I sat by the edge of the road for
some time and cried with pain, I had no idea how I would get
home. But the fact is that an old Volvo cruised by and picked
me up and I was driven all the way home in a green-and-
black Volvo. The driver was very nice and I invited him in for
a cup of tea. We've been married for twenty years now and
have three children, and swapped the Volvo for an electric car
a long time ago, we're both high school teachers, he teaches
electronics and I teach Norwegian and history.

The end.

THE MATIONAL NUSEUM

Today I was woken by a nightmare. Outside, the snow was falling thick and fast, it was really coming down, and it wasn't yet light. I put my feet down on the floor to feel that it was there, I saw that the suit I'd collected from the dry cleaner the day before was hanging on a clothes hanger on the wardrobe door so I wouldn't take the wrong one; it had to be *this* suit. The shoes were standing ready below the suit, so everything was there. In brief: the floor was there, the suit was hanging, the shoes were standing, everything was as it should be. In my dream, on the other hand, I was in the brand-new national museum, of which, also in my dream, I was the director. I took a final round to check that everything was in place for the grand opening, passed through all the rooms in the new, monumental nuseum, made from slate, without windows, only to discover window after window that I had never seen before. The whole point, I thought, was that the building would have no windows, but here they were, popping up, one after another, the sharp light coming in through the glass, into the art, and shining directly on *The Scream* by Edvard Munch, which immediately started to crack, in the way that ice on water splinters to create hairline channels when one surprises oneself by stepping on a place where the ice is too thin. Then I discovered that *The Scream* was hanging upside down. I looked around frantically; Munch's paintings were all hanging upside down. I started to run through room after room: all the art was hanging upside down. The worst was perhaps Bibi Lauf's masterwork, *Gripping Arm*, the five-meter-long lifelike arm that stretched from one end of the room diagonally up toward the ceiling at the other end of the room, where the hand appeared to be gripping something that wasn't there. It was a depiction of how Lauf experienced giving birth, she said—many people who are not familiar with Lauf's explanation understand it rather as the hand reaching up to catch something in the sky and pull it down. God, for example. The way the hand is shaped into such a firm grip means that if it's God the hand is trying to catch, then God must look pretty much like an apple that one might try to pick from a branch. Or a light bulb that has to be twisted out of a ceiling fitting. And all of this falls naturally within the scope of interpretation for *Gripping Arm*. But for Lauf, the truth was that her child had been turned around in the birth canal by the midwife's firm hand, so she came out the right way, and it was such a powerful experience for Lauf, she said, as though she were just a body around a grasping hand, that she wanted to re-create it, with a hand reaching up toward the ceiling to grasp something. In the Lauf Room, *Gripping Arm* was upside down and so looked as though it was trying to grasp something in the ground, to twist it out. In terms of culture, we know only too well what lies hidden down there. I stood petrified, yes, precisely that, and looked at the grasping hand, which assumed a more ominous symbolism, hanging as it was, I felt that civilization itself was at risk, *our time*, yes, that was it, in our time, because was that not what we were doing, here and now in 2020, twisting the beast out of the ground? I was once again gripped by Lauf's piece, I stood there in the Lauf Room and felt everything fall into place, despite the fact that everything was upside down. But then I saw something gray slip past the doorway into the next room, and I had to go see what it was, and it was a huge wolf, and he had a head where his tail should have been, and a tail where his head should have been, and he walked away from me with yellow, staring, almost doomed eyes, perhaps because he would have liked to eat me, but had to follow his tail, which was going the other way, and the only thing I could think of was Olav H. Hauge's poem about a black-clad minister's wife who appears unexpectedly at the farm, "and a yellow wolf," and that I've never understood it, other than that yellow meant danger. And suddenly he stopped, because he'd noticed something, possibly, and then I noticed

it too, it was as though we were in an elevator: the building
was sinking. I looked out through the window and saw the
cranes and skyscrapers disappear over us. I started to run,
past *Gripping Arm*, past *The Scream* and all Munch's upside-
down art, out from the main entrance, and I stood there and
saw, indisputably, the building sink into the earth, the entire,
monumental slate building, until only a meter was left above
ground. It was so mesmerizing to watch it sink, in the way
that it's always, by definition, mesmerizing to watch things
sink, that I felt nothing, neither panic nor despair. And then
I saw a light shining in front of me, from the white neon
letters I'd had made in England. They said: MATIONAL NUSEUM.
There and then, I felt that it simply couldn't be true. Mational
Nuseum! There was something wrong, I could feel it! We had
checked the spelling on the front of the building and on all
the paperwork with our logo, none of the letters had been
switched around, all the letters should be in the right place
and say that this was the Mational Nuseum, Mation, Nus, oh,
to quote my inner life directly, now the letters wouldn't even
let me think the correct word, I howled inside and dashed
toward the opening I had just emerged from, of which there
was now only one meter left, I had to lower myself down
toward the floor and jump, then I ran to my office in the
administration wing, it happened with remarkable speed, as
it often does in dreams, and I looked frantically through all
the papers that I could find, to check: and there it was, it

said "Mational Nuseum" on everything. When I woke up and saw the snow falling thick and fast outside, I was relieved, relieved that it was just a nightmare, relieved that the floor was stable, that my suit was where it should be, that my shoes stood ready, and I was prepared to go to work and inspect all the rooms and check that everything was in place ahead of the grand opening. I got dressed and walked to the nuseum, expecting to find it just as it had been before I dreamed all this: towering many meters above the ground, slate gray and monumental and windowless. But in the distance, through the whirling white, I saw the faint light of some letters. They spelled out the name MATIONAL NUSEUM. The letters shone about a meter from the ground, and not fifteen meters up, as I had expected. I walked through the snow and finally stood there in front of my nuseum: it really had sunk into the ground. I went to where I thought the opening would be, and just as in my dream, only the top part of the main entrance was visible. I looked for the app to unlock the doors and luckily, the doors slid open.

That was twenty minutes ago, so not much time has passed, and no one else has arrived yet. The initial feeling of catastrophe has been replaced by a kind of productive euphoria. I think that with a couple of simple changes, I can rewrite some key points in my speech. I will call the entrance an innovative solution. I will focus on "the transformative power of art." I will say that I am one hundred percent certain that even though the mational nuseum sticks up only one meter above the ground, so we all have to crawl in through a narrow gap and then lower ourselves down, or jump, depending on our physical abilities, then that is what we will do! I will finish by saying: Because we are a mation of art lovers.

THE NORDICS SEEN FROM THE OUTSIDE

We would like to say that the Nordics look like keys on a key ring (or, more precisely, that Scandinavia looks like keys on a key ring), with a couple of larger and smaller splotches of pancake batter around it. We would like to point out that the Nordics are made up of Denmark, Sweden, Norway, Finland, Iceland, Greenland, the Faroes, and Åland. When they are shown on a map, they are often drawn in blue. Scandinavia, which is made up of Norway, Denmark, and Sweden, is darker blue, whereas the rest of the countries that make up the Nordics are lighter blue. Why couldn't they have been shown in dark pink and the others in light pink? What kind of feelings would we then have for the Nordics? We understand that a shade of blue is chosen because the very name *the Nordics* instills a feeling of cold. It's often cold in the Nordics. So cold that your skin shudders at the thought.

On many a cold morning in the Nordics, people have woken and had to light the fire with chattering teeth and shivering, winter-dry fingers. Often, they have had to sit by the fire for hours until it is sufficiently warm beyond the range of the fire for them even to consider moving and starting to make breakfast. But if pink had been chosen as the color to illustrate the Nordics, or orange and yellow, would that really have changed anything? Would we then have automatically started to think of the Nordics as a desert region and visualized the people who live there as being sweaty and hot? No matter what color, our favorite country in the Nordics is Iceland. Iceland looks like a country that's having fun. There's something about the way Iceland looks, as if it were on its way to Greenland. From the outside, Iceland looks like a little fairy-tale creature with a small head and a round body, and we would say that Iceland looks like it's setting merrily off on an adventure. We wonder if it's all the boiling and bubbling that we know is there in Iceland that generates this feeling of exuberant terrificness. Great pillars of water can, as we know, often leap up unexpectedly from warm springs, volcanoes can boil over, hot springs can make the mud burst with big, interesting bubbles. Greenland, on the other hand, has something big and mysterious about it, a feeling of magnitude, one often flies over Greenland on the way to the United States, and then, half-asleep, one might think that Greenland really is enormous and a strangely stable and solid landmass, one seems to fly over Greenland for hours, which is good, as one thinks it is better to have Greenland below than the Atlantic, as one feels it would be better in the case of an emergency landing to land on Greenland rather than the Atlantic, which is known to be home to both sharks and whales, and if we were really unlucky, we could end up in seriously deep water, where we might meet a giant squid. We now seem to be moving away from the Nordics in our mind. This happens as soon as one sees the Nordics from the outside, one discovers the oceans that border the Nordics and one is likely to shift one's gaze to see where one might end up if one were to take the sea route, and one ends up somewhere totally other than the Nordics. It's a trick that the Danish (and Nordic) poet Inger Christensen has used to full effect in the poem "so here I stand by the Barents Sea" in the collection *alphabet*. It's about an I who is standing by the Barents Sea one evening in June, and in the course of the poem's fifty-five lines, we take a trip all the way around the globe, by means of the I tirelessly pointing out what lies behind one geographical area after another, as though she is spinning a globe: "out there is the Barents Sea / and it looks like the Barents Sea / is always alone with the Barents Sea / but around behind the Barents Sea / the water stops at Spitzbergen / and just behind Spitzbergen / ice drifts in the Arctic Ocean," etc., before she spins back to her starting point, which is that she is standing by the Barents Sea on the evening of June 24. And that's how she manages to convey that we're all somehow linked. But back to the subject: *the Nordics* seen from the outside. Seen from the outside, *the Nordics* is a beautiful name, we would say, if we see the name from the outside, we see an *N*, an *o*, an *r*, a *d*, an *i*, a *c*, an *s*. All perfectly normal and frequently used letters in the alphabet. Seen from the outside, the name *the Nordics* is a noun, in the definite form, we can say. In the indefinite, *the Nordics* would be *Nordics*. It would be strange if the Nordics were spoken of as simply Nordics. Then we wouldn't sound like a geographical area at all, but more a group of haphazard, frozen individuals, and any sense of co-herence would fall apart.

What was it that made us want to see the Nordics from the outside? Oh, we can't remember! Sometimes memory is like a black hole. We felt a need to look at the Nordics on a map, to get an overview, and now we've done that. But it makes us wonder all the same. The analysis department lies in the sop-orific half-light that sometimes fills the office after five in the afternoon in the Nordics. Someone is using the photocopier in the copy room to copy an enormous compendium. The coffee machine emits a still click in the common room, and the fridge hums quietly. What was it we wanted to do? And who are we? The wonder that these questions create will soon spill over into frustration, so why did we give them space, why do they tear ahead like two angry but perfectly on-track trains through the forest? The frustration will naturally dissolve into despair, aha, that was why we wanted to see the Nordics from the outside, we did not want to stay in the midst of our own despair, we wanted to lift our gaze. To see the Nordics, where we are, after all, from the outside. We wanted to imagine that the Nordics (or at least Scandinavia) looked like the keys on a key ring. Such physical manifestations can be a deterrent against the feeling of uncontained helplessness. The feeling becomes manifest, something small one can carry and see from the outside. It's just that the keys on a key ring clink in our pocket when we walk, and half remind us of the Barents Sea breaking against something. We can clearly visualize that the something that stops the Barents Sea is a post in Inger Christensen's poem that Inger Christensen has not noticed. It's a solitary post positioned in the water beyond a jetty. The Barents Sea crashes and crashes against this post. We refuse to believe that we, the analysis department, are that post.

We stand up and open the door to the common room. We see the city below—because our office is so high up—glittering and twinkling. We sit down on the windowsill and hear the photocopier fall silent. Now there is a hum as quiet as only an open office can hum when there's no one there. A bit like the hum between two people who are no longer going to be in a relationship together. Just as that hum can fill an office in the Nordics, it can fill you.

And that, unfortunately, is the conclusion of this analysis.

LEECHES ON
THE WRONG TRACK

What could be said about these leeches, which had suctioned themselves onto a fiber-optic cable that had been laid in a forest and through a lake where they lived, other than that they were on the wrong track? They sliced their way through the fiber-optic cable fibers with the tiny razor-sharp calcium teeth in the three jaws inside their two sucker mouths at each end of their leech bodies and sucked out all the thin strands of glass fiber, which carried vast amounts of information that was of no personal use to them. They sucked the fiber-optic cables with such vigor that there was little to indicate that these leeches had done anything else in their lives other than attach themselves onto fiber-optic cables, they were almost professional. One of the leeches was interviewed on TV a month later, and everyone who saw her was

struck by her beauty. She had grown much bigger, almost to
the size of a human being, and her leech body, which had
previously been blackish gray with a zigzag pattern on the
back like a red track, was now transparent and glass-like
and various colors passed through her in waves as she explained that glass and information were now the latest big
thing for leeches. You might not believe it, she said, but one
could actually buy leeches in the pharmacy for medicinal
purposes up until 1959. One could buy leeches! She shook
her leech head in indignation. I know this because of my new
fiber-optic condition, I have access to all the information, it
streams through me in full, so to speak, at all times of day
and night. The anchorman was obviously uncomfortable and
not used to interviewing leeches. And they . . . he said, were
also used for bloodletting, is that not the case? Yes, said the
leech, we were put on bodies that were sick, because the
doctors back then believed it was the blood that was sick, so
we had to suck it out of the body. We know all this now, said
the leech, before we were just bloodsuckers, annelids about
fifteen to twenty centimeters long, with a body divided into
thirty-three segments, like other annelids, who sucked blood
when the opportunity arose. We moved around in ponds
and lakes in our characteristic leech way, which may bring
to mind a kind of primordial soup, if there were creatures
in primordial soup, they would certainly have been leeches,
hahaha, the leech laughed.

How the leeches got back on track, we don't actually know, the only thing we do know is that they stopped eating fiber and went back to blood, and that they were happier for it. That's to say—we can only surmise this, it's not always the case that one has all the information as to why something has transformed from one thing into another, sometimes things change suddenly without a long chain of natural evolution, we don't actually know that they were happy about it, but we can assume so, as there were no more fiberglass-like leeches on the news. Whatever the case, it's a mystery to us why they stopped sucking fiber-optic cables, which is annoying as well, because every time we wade out into a lake and swim around, we have that old fear of leeches once again. Like now: we sit here on a small towel and look at our girlfriend, Anita, where she's standing in a red stripy fifties bathing suit by a lake in the forest, and the sunlight plays on her hair and the water, making everything glitter, but she looks at us and crosses her arms over her chest and says: Eh, no. She doesn't want to swim.

BY THE SHACK

We hadn't eaten anything for three days when a dead man floated past on the river. Karolina looked at the two of us. Her face was gaunt, but also radiated a vigor that the lack of food had not managed to strip from her. She grabbed the rake that lay abandoned on the ground, and started to run. What are you waiting for, she shouted, come on! We tried to run, but were far too weak. Then Harriet said: The lack of food is making us lose our minds, we've got a rubber dinghy in the shack! I visualized the rubber dinghy, it was orange. We walked as fast as our tired bodies could carry us, back to the shack, pulled out the rubber dinghy, saw that it was tired as well, but decided that it would hold at least one of us. It has to be you, I said, I can't swim. Okay, Harriet said, so I helped her push the boat down the gentle slope to the river and carry it over the sandbank, then Harriet climbed in. I'll walk down toward you, I said.

I saw Karolina up ahead, she'd gone out into the river and was wading with the rake held out in front of her, she threw it out, pulled it back, threw it out, pulled it back. Then I saw her raise her fists in fury, having thrown the rake down onto the sandbank, it looked like the dead man had started to drift closer to the other bank. Harriet was on her way down toward Karolina, the man sailed on; Harriet was our only hope now. Hope for what, though? I thought as I watched Harriet disappear down the river and Karolina standing there with her exasperated body language and long, wild red hair that was almost a perfect color extension of the hay-golden plains that ran down to the yellow muddy river. What are we actually going to do with him? I asked Karolina when I reached her, barely able to talk because I was so worn out. Eat him, what do you think? Karolina said. We can't eat a man, I said. What are we going to eat, then, Karolina said, each other? She looked at me with such hunger in her eyes that I had to look at the ground. No, you're right, Karolina, a dead man is all that we need, I said. You and your sense of humor, Karolina said, and gave me a look that I think said, If you don't watch yourself now, I'll eat you. We watched Harriet as she sailed on down the yellow muddy river, under the scorching sun, between the grass plains that stretched out in front of us, dusty and parched.

Harriet. I met Harriet in elementary school, we were in the same class from Class One through to Class Seven, but then she moved, and I didn't see her again until we were adults. She always had the same lunch in her lunchbox: three pieces of crispbread, salami, and a peeled carrot. She'd had the same lunchbox from Class One to Class Seven, she wondered if I could remember it, it had been such an embarrassment for her, to have the same blue metal lunchbox with a clown on it, when the rest of us got new ones every year. I couldn't remember the box, I could remember only what she had in it. She was almost disappointed. I met Karolina at university. I could never decide whether I liked her or didn't like her. She was Swedish, and always contrary. No matter what the lecturers were lecturing on, she was always in opposition and questioned everything. It was annoying. She thought that everyone in this country was intellectually way behind, and did her best to raise us up to her level, or at least make us aware of how far behind we were. But this contrariness could also let her blow her nose loudly on the bus, and she had nostrils that could make as much noise as those of an old man, and exaggerated nose-blowing on the bus was fun. Then one had to like her all the same. And she always knew what to do. If one found oneself in a pickle, Karolina was the person to call. When we, as the only survivors of a plane crash two months ago in the middle of nowhere (here), crawled out of the burning wreckage, it was Karolina who organized everything, going through all the luggage to look for food and medicine and tools. Harriet and I just did as we were told, and tried not to question why the three of us, specifically, had survived, the three of us who knew one another and had bumped into one another coincidentally at the airport, but had sat in different parts of the airplane. We were all forty-three. We all wrote books. It would have been easier to explain if we'd all been sitting in the same row, Harriet said, then it could have been something do with gravity or suchlike, the breaking point of the plane or whatever, that saved us. Karolina just snorted. It's pure coincidence, she said, that's life. None of us said a word about the three rakes that stood leaning up against the wall of the small shack we found after walking through the endless dry yellow grass for a day.

I watched Harriet out on the river, how she was trying to steer the boat over toward the other bank by leaning heavily to the left. Yes! Great idea! Karolina shouted. Come on, Harriet! Thē floating man . . . The last thing we had discussed before falling asleep the night before, lying on our mattresses made from grass, beneath the stars that made that strange clicking sound we'd gotten used to them making, as though someone were turning a kaleidoscope of different heavenly spheres so that the stars clicked into place in different stellar formations, was invisible impressions on the imagination. That the things one reads make a mark, leave traces that one does not always recognize. We discussed the danger of using whatever we had read in our own work in the belief that it was completely new. Karolina had commented acerbically that I'd written a short story about a man who floated upstream, shoe soles first, against the current. She'd found the same motif in a short story by George Blaunders, and another by Loretta David. *Exactly* the same motif as in my text. I haven't read those short stories! I said. There is also, but you obviously don't know about it, I said, a story by Kafka, where a person floats against the current. I read it long after I'd written my own story about the floating man, and was quite taken aback. It's also a surprise to hear that the others have used the same motif. There may be completely other reasons why things like that happen, that several authors write about the same thing, without knowing about one another, Harriet said. Maybe it's a kind of primeval association in the brain. For example, we like to think in opposites. We know that no one floats against the current, we know that no one can fly, so we imagine that we can. And literature, if we see literature as a social contributor, is, as a rule, in opposition to something, rebelling against what is generally accepted, do you follow? To allow someone to float against the current is a good image of that, don't you think? Her face took on a bitter expression, Harriet, who was never bitter, Harriet, who was just Harriet. Most authors I know are so caught up in opposition that it's almost comical, Harriet said. I was once at an event with two authors, they were going to discuss something as basic as writing routines. And the one said the opposite of what the other had said all the time. I write in the morning, said one. Oh, I write at night, said the other. Things have to be tidy around me, said one. Oh, I need to have a mess, said the other. Like two obstreperous young teenagers! It was . . . fucking awful, in fact, Harriet said, and then suddenly we heard the intense clicking sound above us, and we could see some stars pull together, move and turn in clicks into different formations until finally they formed the Big Dipper. None of us said anything, it was too incredible. Have you noticed something, Karolina said, I think it's the most frightening thing about this place—there are no crickets, there's no cricket song at dusk. Normally, in a place like this, with grass like this and a river like that, the sound of crickets would be deafening. As if *you* know where we are, Harriet said. No, but, Karolina said, and we didn't interrupt her now, as her face fell into soft, reminiscing folds, and we'd never seen that before. What was going on, Harriet was bitter and Karolina was soft? Karolina looked around. She looked at the shack behind us, where we'd gathered all the things we'd managed to drag with us. She looked at the river below. She looked at the plains. Don't you recognize it? she said suddenly, I know where we are, I know where we are! Where are we? Harriet asked, eager to know. We're in the children's book by Janosch about the little tiger and the little bear, we're in the story where they try to get to Panama, Karolina said. Harriet and I exchanged glances, we both knew very well that we were not in a Janosch picture book, I remembered the story about the little tiger and the little bear who live on a big plain by a river, and one day a banana crate floats past on the river with PAN-AMA written on the outside, so they decide to go there, but end up going in a circle, they end up back on the plain by the river, and nothing here, except for the endless plain and the river, was anything like it. We really are, Karolina said, and stood up, with shining eyes, this is the house where they live (she pointed at the shack), they were raking the grass and tidying up (she pointed to the rakes that we'd leaned against the wall for the night), and there is the river that twists and turns through the grassy landscape. And Janosch always has yellow tones! I read the book to Kalle just before I left! Kalle was Karolina's four-year-old son. Karolina, I said, we should sleep now. Karolina sat down again on her grass mattress and stared at the river. I just know it, she said. She resembled a statue there in the dark, she was sitting so still. That's what this all means, she said, starting up. We're all characters in one an-other's stories, this is most probably a text that's been posted online where we're separate links to other stories, like hyper-text, which means that if we click on one another, we'll move on to the next story, let's try! she said, frantically, and looked at us. Click on me! Neither of us tried to click on her, so she cautiously reached out her hand and touched me, tried to click on me, as though I were a link. Nothing happened. Karolina lay down on the mattress without saying a word.

Shortly afterward she fell asleep, with a long sigh, as though the breath of life had left her there on the mattress. Harriet and I lay awake, Karolina lay on the outside, Harriet was in the middle, and I was on the other side of Harriet. We heard a faint rumbling, Harriet turned toward me, making the hay rustle. It's just Karolina's stomach, I said, mine is rumbling all the time. Why has this happened, Harriet said. The thought of Janosch and Kalle had made us sad. Who knows, I said. I think about how petty my worries were before. For example, for the past ten years I've been annoyed that not one of the critics who read my last essay collection commented on the epigraph. I tried to laugh, but nothing came out. What did it say, then, Harriet said, and swiftly apologized and said she hadn't read it. That's fine, I said, I haven't read your books either. Harriet smiled a small, tired smile before she fell asleep. I lay there alone and imagined a dialogue between Harriet and me. But what did it say? said Harriet in the imagined dialogue. It said: "is someone coming toward me on the road, am I sitting with my face turned toward someone? RSVP," I said. What does *RSVP* mean again, Harriet said. It means please reply, as in RSVP on an invitation. Then I explained it all to Harriet, how I had thought that if this quote from Inger Christensen were at the beginning of the essay collection, the reader would understand that the essays were written by someone who was looking for answers from somebody sitting on the other side of the table, as is the case in any everyday situation where one person is sitting on the other side of a table from another. That I was writing with uncertainty, but in the hope that there was someone on the other side. That my text was an invitation, in a way. That I was hoping I would get an answer. That someone would come. But that there was a risk that no one would answer, and I was sitting at the table alone. But no one noticed it, how ironic is that, I imagined I said, and heard the stars click again, and above I saw the stars click into place to form Orion. Ah, I thought, they clicked because I thought the word *ironic*, before they clicked when Harriet said "fucking awful," I said "fuck" out loud, but nothing happened, I said "the irony of fate," and all was quiet, I said "hell," but not even a hint of a click. The pitch-black and twinkling starry sky stretched over us, and while the others slept I thought about this, that we wanted someone to come, that we wanted coherence, that we could feel that the slightest rustling in the reeds was one natural phenomenon talking to another, in other words you, that all this grass was trying to say something, that the stars were trying to say something, that we were not alone. That's why people suddenly pop up who float against the current in a river, I thought, that's what it was about, not only *opposition*, but even more, *response*! And then I fell asleep.

Up ahead we could see Harriet waving and waving at us with one hand, while she held the other one down in the water.

Holy shit, Karolina said, she's got hold of him, she's actually managed. Oh, do you think so, I said, reluctantly, as, deep down, I really didn't want to eat a dead man, I had absolutely no intention of eating that person, even if I had to eat grass for the rest of the future, I would rather eat grass. Harriet waved and waved, and while Karolina walked faster and faster, I pulled back and slowed down, I didn't want to know, I didn't want to know any more about it, I didn't want the future to reveal itself, I wanted to stop here, go back, sit down by the shack, rake a little more around the shack, start to look for more materials to make a roof, do exactly what we had been doing before this person came along and spoiled it all.

DIGRESSIVE FIT

This bear, who was stealthily making his way toward the perfect prey, namely a deer that was standing completely still and eating, got distracted when he passed a blueberry patch. We all know how much bears love blueberries, and this was, sadly for him, a bear who was easily distracted. The fact was that he simply had to try the blueberries, and when he looked up after a few minutes of ecstatic guzzling and discovered that the deer was gone, he hit his forehead with the heel of his paw and groaned: Oh no, not another digressive fit! He really had to stop this. He carried on through the forest with a blue nose and grumbled in irritation at the challenges his personality presented.

This is all true, we who are telling you this are a cloud of midges who can read thoughts, and who have often swarmed around this delightful bear. If you have ever wondered, when a cloud of midges swarms around your head while you're lying on a lounge chair trying to sunbathe, why we make that faint humming sound, it's because we're reading your thoughts. It is the sound of your own thoughts that you hear. You might want to think about that the next time you slice a kitchen knife through a cloud of midges that are swarming around you as you sit trying to cut some bread, early one morning in a campsite in Finland.

SLIME EELS IN THE DARK

This is a play that will soon be over. We see an old dirt road, and on the dirt road is a cart with a heavy load, and a young woman who picks something up from the ground that she puts in what we could also call the wagon. It's dark, because it's evening. This means that we almost can't see the road, which disappears into a forest on what seems to be the backdrop, only it isn't, because, we forgot to say at the start, we're not on a stage, we are in reality. This is reality. Now we notice that there's a man standing in the middle of the road behind the wagon, and a horse standing there as well. It's completely silent, no one makes a sound, not even the horse. Because it is so tangibly quiet, our ears start to listen intently, and what we then perceive is simply revolting: we can hear, as if the sound is emerging from our very soul, something slimy and viscous squelching against something else, as though hundreds of snakes were twisting and writhing in a pit, and that is because the wagon is in fact full of slime eels. Until now we thought it was too dark to see what the pile on the cart was, but now that our eyes are more accustomed to the dark, we can see it: the anthill-like pile on the cart is writhing with something that wriggles—and as we know, it's slime eels. Oh, the young woman says now, so loud that we jump. We see the man standing on the other side, and he leans toward the wagon as though to tip it over. She stands behind him and says: Please can you not tip my load of slime eels onto the road? Then she says that she's spent a long time collecting them, diving for them, carrying them in buckets, carefully emptying them out into the back of the wagon. Her plan now is to harness the horse to the wagon and then start the journey home and so be home just before midnight. She has a lantern that she will hang from a tall stick on the wagon, which will light her way so she won't drive off the road, and if the lantern doesn't work, she will hang up a slime eel, which will then feel threatened and so produce a lot of slime on which she can then shine her cell phone so the light reflects onto the road. She has thought of everything. Please, she says. And then has her longest speech, her voice barely audible over the sound of the writhing eels: "It would be unbearable for me if you tipped this load over now and all the slime eels slithered off in every direction in the dark and I had to crawl around on all fours to find them, grab them, and carry them back to the cart, basically start to gather all the slime eels again." Goodness, how strange that we don't know where she comes from, why she is gathering slime eels, and how she ended up in this bizarre situation where she has to argue with him not to tip over her cartload! What's the meaning of all this, why do people just stand in the road with wagons and horses and talk, questions we can imagine several overdimensioned, indignant mouths with black lipstick hanging over this scene might ask. He might, for example, say this now: But it's been several days since I last tipped over a cartload. To which she replies: But, oh, *must* you! And he argues that she has to think of him as well in all this. He claims he's dependent on tipping over cartloads. "I live for it," he says with passion. "The feeling one gets when one sees a cartload fall over and whatever is in the cart spills out onto the road and creates havoc for whoever owns it," he says, "there is *little* or *nothing* that can compare with that. It releases all these endorphins in me and makes me a better person, I'm happier, I think more clearly, it's a bit like a shower, tipping over a loaded cart." Sadly, this is her reply: "I understand, but—" and he interrupts her and says, "Just because you stand here trying to win sympathy, because you've struggled and toiled to gather all this up, doesn't mean it's worth more than the endorphins that are released in me, and maybe I won't feel the need to tip over another cart for several days! Think of all the others you're sparing when I tip over this cartload." Then he tips over the cartload. And here, the short play, which we see is called *Slime Eels in the Dark*, comes to an end. It ends with the young woman lying on her stomach on the road trying to gather the slime eels that are slithering and wriggling in all directions, into the forest and everywhere, and with the man walking home happy and relieved. Too many stories end like this, and we hope that we've now done our bit to draw attention to this, that things must not end like this, that there must be other endings, endings other than slime eels slithering silently away.

SHORT MONSTER ANALYSIS

Siv will no doubt always associate the beautiful small leaf hut in the park with the fact that she laughed scornfully at his innermost pain. The leafy branches wove together to create a roof, the grass was the floor, and the festival had put a big screen and a few benches in there to make a small cinema, and there was a livestream from the concert hall out into the park. There were no people sitting on the benches in the leaf hut, but there were four hundred people in the auditorium, and he was sitting on the stage talking about life and music and had reached so deep into his own psyche that the pain poured out and made him cry. But here in the park, it was only his face on the big screen in a small leaf hut. It was when his voice faltered and a small sob came out instead of a word that Siv laughed as she passed the leaf hut and heard his familiar voice, which she had not heard in twenty years; her laughter was loud and scornful, without a thought.

She had prepared herself for the fact that now, twenty years later, they would inevitably bump into each other, she had seen in the festival program that they were both going to perform. Siv felt no need to meet him ever again, she was happy that he was living his life, she was living hers, and even though she sometimes fantasized that he'd summoned her, her alone, out of all the lovers he had lured in before stabbing them through the heart, to his deathbed to tell her that he had understood what a terrible person he had been and could she forgive him, and that he had thought about her all his life, in reality, she did not want to meet him again, but the very first people Siv met, as she stood at the reception desk to check in to the festival hotel, were him and his wife. They pretended not to see her; she pretended not to see them.

But twenty years had passed! How about finally embracing it in her own response pattern and not behaving like someone with a bleeding and ridiculously open trauma? Siv was living another life, after all. She was loved for who she was, by people whom she loved in return. People out there in reality. Twenty years should be enough time to forgive and look at things with a bigger heart. But that's the way it is, she thought as she walked on toward the café, she *laughed* when she heard him talking about his innermost pain, which she remembered only too well, as he spoke of pretty much nothing else when they were together, she laughed when she heard it on an outdoor screen under some trees. Siv understood something about herself that she perhaps had not realized before, but now knew, that she was cold, she could laugh at someone else's pain. And that was, by definition, no matter how deeply one had been hurt by somebody, not nice. Pain was pain, no matter what Siv thought of it. And yet her spontaneous response was laughter! Oh, complex problem!

But was it perhaps the situation, that he was talking on a *big screen* in a small and intimate leaf hut, with *benches where other people could have sat and listened*, but they were empty, was it perhaps the *mismatch* that made her laugh, the incongruity of the visuals, *his pain on the big screen in a small leaf hut*? Yes, maybe, she thought, as she walked toward the café and tried to pick apart what had just happened, so she could understand it. And was it perhaps the case that she linked his pain on the big screen in the small, empty leaf hut with her own situation twenty years ago, when she sat, in all her inexperience, with a grown, crying man? PAH, she knew that it wasn't the visual incongruity that had provoked the laughter, it was *she*, it was *she* who laughed, at him sitting and crying on the stage, that was the truth, plain and simple: she thought her former lover was pathetic, that was the reason. And he had used his innermost pain to generate sympathy in those few weeks when their passions had raged, twenty years ago, in the same way that he was using this pain now, on the stage, in front of four hundred people.

Otherwise, the hotel was lovely and very Nordic. But for one of the musicians, a highly respected pianist from Eastern Europe, it was unbearable. They walked down the corridor together after a dinner, and he pointed to a rustic carved chair that stood alone by a window and said: Oh, it's too Scandinavian. Another evening she saw the same pianist sitting in one of the armchairs in the hotel lobby, surrounded by admirers, he had a happy smile on his face, and was elaborating on this or that. Her room was spacious and had a balcony that faced a large forest. On the first night, Siv spotted a spider in a web up in the right-hand corner of the room. It was right under the ceiling, too high for her to reach. But because it was a fair way from there over to the bed, she reckoned that the spider would not be able to spin all the way over, that it had found its small corner in the big room, and would stay there. She was terrified of spiders, but knew this much: they liked their webs. And that proved to be the case. It stayed in its corner for the three days that she was there.

Pull yourself together, Siv thought, back in the situation where she had just laughed out loud at another person's real pain, livestreamed on a big screen in a small leaf hut. Why is it that one does not wish well those who have hurt one? How can one become so cold that one laughs at their innermost pain? Is it because one believes that they use their inner-most pain like crocodiles use their tears: to elicit sympathy from . . . Who do crocodiles want to draw sympathy from when they cry? she thought, as she walked toward the café for coffee and a piece of apple cake, she had to google "crocodile tears" because she had no idea where the term came from, only that crocodile tears didn't happen in reality, in the way that the term is used, because, if one thought about it, it was unlikely that crocodiles would need sympathy from any living creature, and if there were situations where crocodiles were the weaker party, it would surely be in confrontation with other crocodiles, *whoosh*, the tears trickled from the cor-ner of crocodile eyes, *spare me, spare me*? But it turned out that the saying about crocodile tears, or so her smartphone told her, came from the belief that crocodiles made a sound a bit like a baby crying in order to lure people to them so they could eat them. But that was a myth. However, they did actu-ally shed tears when they ate, scientists had discovered. The tears were probably the result of all the huffing and puffing crocodiles did when they ate, pressing the air out through the sinuses, and this air then probably mixed with the tears in the crocodiles' lachrymal glands as they chewed, and was squeezed out through the eyes. She felt it was uncomfortably appropriate. He was sitting in there on the stage guzzling their sympathy, his insides huffing and puffing as his big sharp teeth chewed and ate; out streamed the tears.

It won't let me, Siv thought as she sat there, eating her apple cake and looking out at the sea. No matter how I try to analyze my own reaction, I cannot unpick the monster. Which is me, after all, not him. Because only a monster could laugh at someone else's pain. She had to google "monster." It turned out that the word *monster* came from the Vulgar Latin verb *monstrare*, which meant to point out or show. Thus, as a noun, something that lets itself be pointed out or puts itself on display. There was only a small amount of cream left on her plate now. The sea was light blue, the sky was light blue, a few wispy white clouds lay on the horizon. Her denim jacket was light blue, her nails were orange, her hands were hooves, her tongue was split, and her heart was black and beating as she got up to go to the toilet.

So, it is plain to see that Siv is a monster. There was no need to take a detour into her innermost life. We could simply have looked in her mouth and seen her split tongue, and spared ourselves an entire story.

A VISIT TO MONK'S HOUSE

Alcea was the first to write on Tripadvisor. She wrote that she was planning a little visit to Monk's House, the home of Virginia and Leonard Woolf, in Rodmell, 7 kilometers south of Lewes, in East Sussex, England. However, she had a bladder problem and so didn't dare travel until she knew what toilet facilities were available at the house. Because of her bladder problem, there had to be more than one toilet, so she wouldn't need to stand in a queue if she suddenly had to pee, but it would be worse still if there was no toilet there at all. She had read on the website that there was a toilet outside that visitors could use. Was there anyone who knew what it looked like? She imagined, as it was a house from the beginning of the nineteenth century, that it might be one of those toilets with a carving on the door, a half-moon, for example, that it had a low ceiling, and it was to the side of the main house, so one might have to walk some way to get there. Or perhaps, Alcea wrote, it was one of those chemical toilets that were never pleasant to use. She had watched lots of videos on YouTube where people talked about their visit to Monk's House, ever hopeful that she might catch a glimpse of the toilet.

I ate a yogurt as I sat reading this, and I have to say, I was utterly gripped by the problem. I've had a bladder problem myself and know how crucial is it to have a toilet nearby if one is to venture out into the world. But it wasn't only this identification with her bladder problem that captivated me, it was also how she described her longing to visit the house. For example, she wrote that she had seen people on YouTube walk down a road in the rain, the road to Monk's House, they were thoughtful and reverential, with only the slightest swing in their arms. She had seen close-up shots of leaves lying in the roof gutters above the winter garden, and leaves lying on the glass roof of the winter garden, a black-and-white cat stalking across the grass. She had seen what the living room looked like, with its stone floor and armchairs and paintings, the stone floor didn't surprise her, it was not so usual in Norway, perhaps, but she had once been to Brittany and stayed in a house with a similar floor, so she was not completely unfamiliar with brown European stone floors. The floor, Alcea wrote, was often cold, so she wondered how they had heated the house, and what they had had on their feet when they walked around inside, but she could learn about that later,

right now the most important thing was the toilet. And the
toilet was not shown in any of the videos she had seen. She so
yearned, she wrote, to wander around the house and see
everything as it had been when Virginia Woolf was alive. She
longed to stand and watch a long-stemmed flower, for example a rose or a hollyhock, swaying in the summer breeze or
the rain. It was as though the rain on the grass and Virginia
Woolf's hollyhocks meant the world to her. I'd never seen
anyone write anything like it on Tripadvisor, so I was simply
enthralled. She longed for the grass around the house and to
come out of a room that she had seen in one of the films, and
to think: Virginia Woolf once came out here, in exactly this
way, only now it was her. Here she was, very much alive, and
walking through exactly the same door that Virginia Woolf
had walked through. She might even be placing her feet in   —
exactly the same places that Virginia Woolf had placed hers,
who knew, it was impossible to know for sure, wrote Alcea.
But it was the toilet that was most relevant for her, if she was
going to be able to do any of this at all, and she would be des-
perately unhappy if it couldn't be done, if she had to sit in her
own garden all summer and only daydream about Virginia
Woolf's garden, it would just not be the same. She didn't
even have hollyhocks in her garden and she somehow envisaged that Virginia Woolf did, but, Alcea wrote, she might be
wrong, as hollyhocks are biennial. And then someone would
have had to plant the hollyhocks year after year, and some-

one else would have had to take over from them, as it had
been at least two generations since Virginia Woolf died, in
terms of the working life of a gardener, that is; if not, the
gardener who had planted hollyhocks every other year since
her death would now be ancient. Alcea ended by saying: If
anyone has any kind of information about Virginia Woolf's
toilet, please reply.

I was not at all familiar with that part of Great Britain, I had
not read Virginia Woolf, and I didn't know if Virginia Woolf's
house had a toilet, in fact, I had never been to Britain, but
immediately started to search on Google and wrote that even
though I knew the area fairly well, I couldn't say anything
about the toilet facilities, in particular, at Monk's House,
however: the building was part of the National Trust, so one
could safely assume that the toilet was of a relatively good
standard and not horribly primitive. In addition, I wrote that
she would find the email address for Monk's House on the
website, under "Contact Us." I wished her the best of luck.

A whole day passed before she answered. I remember the
day well, nothing happened. I sat and read other posts on
Tripadvisor, but it was all so uninteresting, Algarve, Pyre-
nees, Venice, all I could think about was Virginia Woolf's
toilet. I opened the fridge and saw that there was no yogurt
left, so I went to the shop, but was impatient to get home to

see if Alcea had answered. I saw some bushes swaying in the wind and thought about hollyhocks. I looked at the grass around my block in a different way when I got home: so that's what grass looked like! But there was no answer until the next day. Alcea wrote to thank me. She had written to them, but the house was closed for winter, and she assumed that someone would be checking the email, maybe the gardener? She imagined the gardener sitting in Virginia Woolf's living room in winter, with cold feet, answering emails. She could just imagine what he looked like. He had green Wellington boots and a sixpence cap. It was wet outside and damp inside in winter, and the fact that it was damper now than ever before, not less, was a worry. The gardener had a weathered face, and he sat with the laptop on his lap, and checked the emails that were sent to Monk's House, and it was strange to know, Alcea wrote, that he existed at all, so many years after the people who had lived in the house had gone, that he could sit there like a point in posterity in his green Wellington boots, which perhaps left wet marks on the brown stone floor as he sat there and answered emails about what the toilets looked like. She imagined that he was thinking: Well, I guess one can also ask what the toilet looks like. But what he wouldn't know was that this was of particular importance to her, to whether she would go there or not, whether she would be able to experience walking around in Virginia Woolf's garden, and whether she would be able to see everything that she longed to see. He couldn't know that underlying this rather trivial question about the toilets was a deep yearning.

No, I replied, as I didn't really know what to reply. I regretted it as soon as I hit "send," why couldn't I answer any more than "no"? This small *no* bothered me for weeks, that I had not been able to give a better response, and to say that she had helped me to notice the grass around my block. It bothered me so much that I couldn't face going onto the page to see if she had replied, but eventually, I had to check, and she hadn't, instead there was a post with bad punctuation from someone who, it later transpired, was called Emma:

I've also thought about going to Monks House, have you been there yet. Can you say a little about what it was like but I wondered also about what and how the daybed is.

After this, I went onto the site daily to check if there were any answers, but there was nothing. However, several weeks later, there was a post from someone who later turned out to be called Samantha:

Hello, have you been to Monk's House yet?

So I jumped on as well after a few days, and wrote:

Hello, we're curious to know how you got on, did you find out if there were hollyhocks etc.?

But there was still no response. All was quiet for months. Samantha, Emma, and I all carried the same worry, why had she not answered? Every time I saw the bush I had noticed on the day that I went to the shop to buy yogurt, after I'd read her post, I reflected on her silence. It was as though it was her blowing from inside the bush. Emma, Samantha, and I all more or less simultaneously sent private messages to one another, where we asked one another what we thought had happened to her. And so our internet friendship began, and quickly became very intense. It turned out that we were all Norwegian, and that we all liked to daydream, which was why we were on Tripadvisor, even though we weren't actually going anywhere. Soon we were sharing our deepest, most private thoughts and fears and joys. Emma had a death threat hanging over her, one of the students who had been expelled from the high school where she worked had sent an email to her and threatened her, but Emma wrote that even though this was a real threat, the fear that came from inside and prevented one from showing one's true colors, or doing things one didn't really dare, was worse. She had been so touched by Alcea's question on Tripadvisor about Virginia Woolf's toilet precisely because there was something fearless about it. Samantha countered that it was in fact fear that had prompted Alcea to seek more information on the internet about the toilet, after all, she feared that there was no toilet there at all. And that, in truth, is fearless: to ask for information about what a toilet looks like, said Emma, on the internet, that is, in our small chat group, and I admire Alcea for her fearlessness. I myself had wondered and wondered what she had meant by asking about the daybed, but didn't dare to ask. Emma had also confessed that she'd been very drunk the night she sat there surfing the internet and found Alcea's post about Monk's House, and that was why the syntax in her post was a bit odd. She hadn't meant to get so drunk, but the wine was so good, and it was Friday and she had too many tests to correct that weekend, and on Monday she was going to meet the parents of one of the other students who had sent another death threat. We had replied to this with three laughing faces, both Samantha and I. We were all absolutely certain that if Alcea, as we called her, the Latin term for hollyhocks, was still alive, she would have written an answer on Tripadvisor and told us, because we believed, from what we had read, that she was the sort of person who liked to tell things. Let's go to look for her, Emma wrote one day, then we can meet in real life, and then we can all go on a trip, together! Yes, wrote Samantha, what a fantastic idea. I agreed, with great enthusiasm.

So we decided to go to look for her at Monk's House, but we got no farther than Oslo Airport.

Samantha was the first one I met, at check-in, she was wearing light blue denim and had short blond hair, and in a way, that was that. She had a light brown leather handbag and a dark pink backpack, of the Norrøna variety, a blue rain jacket, and a thin purple woolen snood instead of a scarf. Samantha was in many ways a bit like the question she had asked Alcea: direct and straightforward. "Hello, have you been to Monk's House yet?" We spotted Emma coming toward us from the escalator, we realized immediately that it was Emma, though of course we didn't know. She was dressed in black, black denim, black leather boots, black trench coat, and a black scarf with tassels, with thin shoulder-length brown hair and a lot of makeup. I can't quite explain it, but I noticed that something was making Samantha uneasy, and saw the same thing on Emma's face when she reached us, a kind of twitching in their bodies, as though they recognized each other from their daily lives as soon as they saw each other and had immediately pigeonholed each other.

But the mood was buoyant as we went through security. I hoped, as I stood there sweating in my raincoat, that nothing about me was too disappointing for the other two women, I was a very ordinary man, and I had earphones around my neck. I was wearing blue jeans and sneakers and had a green Norrøna backpack, so Samantha and I were more alike on the outside. But I had felt closer to Emma, on the internet at least. I could completely sympathize with her wish to stand naked and fearless in the face of the world. To really feel that I was filled with inner calm and that nothing was dangerous. "'But when we sit together, close,' said Bernard, 'we melt into each other with phrases. We are edged with mist. We make an unsubstantial territory,'" Emma had written to us, it was a quote from one of Virginia Woolf's novels that neither Samantha nor I had read, and it was how she pictured the three of us in the chat group: We sat close together with sentences, the edges of our bodies enveloped in mist. We three were an unsubstantial landscape. And yet, Emma wrote, we were beautiful.

When I write this now, I realize that it must have been this that made her disappear. We were possible only as long as we were on the internet, where we were sentences and our bodies were enveloped in mist. She, with her black trench coat, must have reacted to our colorful Norrøna rucksacks and blue denim. But still, I didn't think that was enough to forgive the confusion and sorrow that both Samantha and I felt when we went to the duty-free to look for Emma, who we thought had gone to try a Chanel perfume, a green one, as she said she was going to do. There was no Emma there. No Emma at Chanel, Dior, or Versace. No Emma came to the gate. We got the information desk to put out a call and ask her to meet "Elos and Samantha at Gate 23." No Emma came. When I heard our names, and that we were standing by a gate, which was here, it was as though who I really was had dissolved into the mist, and I saw that Samantha was feeling the same where she stood; that we were not standing there, that we were not called Elos and Samantha, not like this. We're not going, are we, Samantha said, and looked at me as she slowly faded into gray before my eyes. No, I barely managed to whisper before the air erased us completely and the gate personnel called for Emma one last time.

I have sometimes wondered if Emma was in fact Alcea. If it was she who wrote the first post on Tripadvisor and commented herself, after I did. If she was playing a game with us, to lure us in and then disappear twice, perhaps she wanted someone to feel that the numbing silence to be found on the internet when someone doesn't answer is the same feeling as when a traveling companion disappears at the airport. At other times, I've wondered if she was killed by one of her students. Neither theory is particularly plausible. But every time I see hollyhocks swaying gently on their long stems in the wind, I'm touched by the feeling of something extraterrestrial and mysterious, as if they had been planted there only to remind me of something.

WISH, DREAM, OBSERVATION

1. I would like a team of horses to cross the river now, so I can film their hooves breaking the surface of the water in slow motion. I want there to be the sound of horses neighing. I want to hear the sound of heavy hooves on a sandbank. I want the horses to start galloping, like in a Western, up the gentle green hillside when they reach the other bank. I want the horses to gallop right to the top of the green hill, and us to reach the top at the same time, and our camera to sweep over the horses and discover, on the other side of the ridge, a valley, where Henrik Ibsen lies, arms and legs splayed like Gulliver, looking up at the miniature horses on top of the miniature hill, with an irritated expression on his face.

2. In a dream, I see the face of Henrik Ibsen rise up over the mountain early one morning. To begin with, I see only the gray hair on the top of his head. Then it rises slowly, I see the furrows in his forehead, his heavy eyebrows, his seri-

ous eyes that stare straight at me, his nose, his characteristic beard, his mouth like a streak in its depths. And finally the entire face of Henrik Ibsen is in the sky like a shimmering silver hologram, shining, like a lonely kelp forest at night.

3. Two academics and an author are sitting on a small stage at a round table with a red velvet curtain as a backdrop. It looks like a scene from a David Lynch film, and what they are discussing is Henrik Ibsen. Henrik Ibsen is not there. The manner in which Henrik Ibsen is not there is all-encompassing. As not-present as a duck, a swan, or a boat that is not floating on a lake. Never has the word *not* been more like Henrik Ibsen. The word *not* floats past us on the water with bushy white whiskers and makes the V sign before disappearing.

THE POINT

The poor girl! You see, everything around her turned
into slime eels. Well, not everything, naturally, but most
things. When she took her physics exam: the exam paper
turned into slime eels. Then the desk turned into slime eels,
and then the chair and then the floor. When she was in a
relationship that she thought was good, and that had not yet
turned into slime eels: her boyfriend turned into slime eels.
When she stood in a cosmetics shop and picked up a bot-
tle of shampoo to have a closer look, as it might help to
deal with her unruly hair that never behaved as it should: it
turned into slime eels. When she sat on the bus to Nesodden
once, on the way to see her little sister, the bus turned into
slime eels, then all the passengers turned into slime eels,
and then, finally, the driver as well. As you probably realize,
these are just a few examples of what turned into slime eels
in her presence. We understand that you might fumble to

find some kind of explanation, as we have done—and might get no further than the rather cold consolation that sometimes in life it feels like everything you touch turns into slime eels. But having scoured various explanation models, we seem to have ended up here: all this actually happened! In the life of this girl, whose experience was that everything around her turned into slime eels, as though any opening was closed by this: slime eels. And when we consider how hard it is for us to accept this simple premise, surely this is peanuts compared with how tired and fed up the girl was with everything turning into slime eels. When will anything just be what it is? she found herself thinking one evening as she stood under a streetlight trying to find out when the next bus home was, on her phone, which immediately started to turn into a slime eel. The very next day, she got an answer, the day she observed a great tit in the forest, and the great tit did not turn into a slime eel. The girl stood quiet as a mouse, terrified that the bird would turn into a slime eel, and watched the great tit peck at an apple on the ground with a pine needle in its beak, and out of the hole in the apple came a grub, not a slime eel, but a grub, which the great tit ate. It was a small bird. Yellow-breasted and black-headed. Small, active, and real. And itself in every moment that the girl stood there. What a joy: something had not turned into a slime eel! After this, she went back to the forest frequently to look for the great tit, and if she was lucky, she would spot it, and *the great tit continued to be the great tit*, a surprisingly stable point, a point she could build her whole life around. As though she were finally sitting at a window and looking out.

THE BACK DOOR

When I was a child, my father saved five baby great tits from an old apple tree, where they had been left in a hole by their parents, who had been killed by our cat. Great tits don't carve out their own nest cavities, they often use holes in rotten trees, or mailboxes, or the hollow insides of lampposts. My father couldn't get them out with his hands, they peeped and gaped with their beaks inside the tree, so he polished and altered an old shoehorn to fit into the tree and then he lifted them out, all five, and put them in a shoebox. He installed them in one of the rooms in the loft, the one with the yellow wallpaper that stood empty. He put out a drying rack, where they could perch when they were big enough, and we fed them with worms and insects. The intention was that they would grow up there in the yellow room, five small great tits, and later fend for themselves in nature. What I remember best, better than all the small bird graves, as the great tit babies died one after the other, is the smell of bird shit and how suddenly they could shit. You could be standing looking at the bird and suddenly: bird shit on the floor, white and smelly, like one of nature's magic tricks.

I thought about them when I watched a nature program the other day, about peculiar creatures that live in the sea. The most peculiar creature, if you ask me, was a fish that could walk on the seabed, and could camouflage itself; it basically looked like a messy stone, full of corals. But it was a fish, a camouflaged sculpin. He puttered along the seabed until he found a group of stones with waving corals that looked just like him, and settled down beside them. Then he lifted, from the top of his head, something that resembled a tiny thin fishing rod, with an oblong white cloth-like bait at the end. All this was the fish. He was a fish with a fishing rod. He now got his fishing rod to vibrate, to catch the interest of smaller fish, so they would approach. He kept the intriguing bait jumping merrily just above his own mouth. When a small stripy blue fish then came close enough, the sculpin sucked the small blue fish into his mouth so quickly that it was easy to miss it. He just swallowed it, as though he were a vacuum cleaner, wiped it from the water's history forever, as though it had never swum there, like the carefree little stripy blue fish it had been, in the same way that the universe, it is said, had suddenly appeared from nothing. Only in reverse.

The fish reminded me of the man who appeared in my life a few months ago, and who made me feel seen. I had longed for this for all of the fifty-two years of my life; I had felt that *I* wasn't seen. For who I was. As though my soul were something that existed, but only I knew about her, and the more time that passed without anyone else seeing her, the more she faded, until I was unsure that she actually existed, this soul, or if she was something I had just made up. The concept of the soul is problematic, I'm aware of that, the Greeks used it as the name for life breath—that which makes us alive—but later it branched out into religious and philosophical discussions that I'm not going to detail here, as it's more than I can do. I haven't exactly paid much attention to the history of the concept of the soul, but rather to the soul's real, beautiful, and often quite painful movements through the human body. Some days I saw my soul as a woman in a purple taffeta dress who disappeared farther and farther down a corridor in my inner life, her head bowed, and light after light was lit on the wall ahead of her, and light after light was extinguished behind her. On other days, unfortunately for me, I envisaged the River Ouse behind Virginia Woolf's house when I thought of the word *soul*, perhaps because of the *ou*. If you think about it, the word *soul* also sounds a bit like a rhyme with *owl*, which has often made me think of the soul as an eagle owl, sitting hidden at dusk. But: then he turned up here and looked at me with such warm and interested eyes, I, who now experienced daily what it meant to be fifty-two, in body, as though I were the most incredible and beautiful creature he had ever seen, with a soul so stunning that he couldn't believe it. I would like to describe it as follows: it was as though everything stood still, and he came flying through the sky like a large gray bird and landed right in front of me and enveloped me in warm, majestic grayness. Yes, I could have described it with such ecstasy. But whatever the case, I remembered who I was when I looked into his eyes. The river started to flow again. The woman in the purple taffeta dress came running down the corridor. The eagle owl opened its eyes. And it was as though he remembered who he was, when he looked into my eyes. I even wrote on a piece of paper, and it sometimes touched me when I read it: We humans must remember each other.

But my point here, today, is not that he came, the point is that he disappeared: one day he was no longer there. As suddenly as he had appeared, he disappeared. I didn't even manage to see him flying backward in slow motion through the sky. He was just gone. All my calls: unanswered. All my texts: sent into an empty darkness. My soul: ah, well. I thought about it just the other day, when I passed a bush growing up against a rock face as I walked home from a spin class, and suddenly heard a rustle, I turned my head and saw a blackbird release a white shit the very second I looked at it, it happened so fast. I wish there were a word that could describe how suddenly blackbirds shit, as suddenly as a camouflaged sculpin sucks in its victims, as suddenly as the universe one day opened up and let me out through a back door I didn't know I had reached.

PROTEST

We herewith protest that the previous text had such an unhappy ending. Unhappy endings drive us nuts, and we think
that people who are let out a back door, without even knowing
they're being shown to the back door, should be given a prize.
Innocent and full of expectation, they have until now believed
that they were being shown to the entrance of a palace or something, and are not prepared to find themselves suddenly outside
a back door, looking down at a sad gravel backyard and the
ugly wobbly metal staircase that leads down to it. Instead, there
should be a big prize of some sort behind the back door, not a
large basket full of fruit and chocolate, as fruit rots so quickly,
nor should it be a bathroom scale, a red geranium, a salt-cured
leg of lamb, a lamp, or a toilet paper roll doll, no matter how
beautiful the pink dress is that's draped over the toilet paper
roll, and a 25,000-krone check is not enough either, but it could,
for example, be a vacation, a car, or maybe even a new house.

We hope our protest will be taken into consideration.

THE NEW POTATOES

Three dead ducks flew right over my head. I could see they were dead, as they were only duck skeletons, but otherwise they behaved as if they were alive. What's the point of that, I thought, why don't the dead just stay on the ground, why do they have to mix with living ducks like that, appropriate the qualities of the living ducks and behave as if nothing has happened, flying like they were alive over my head and whistling, aha, they were goldeneyes, making their famous whistling sound, dead goldeneyes, three of them, that now disappeared into the horizon, almost melted into the sky because of the whiteness of their bones, the see-throughness of the skeleton and the steadily increasing distance.

I continued to dig in the earth. There were many more potatoes than I had even dared hope. It surprised me, every year, that the small tubers that I planted in early spring could multiply into so many potatoes, small pale faces or finger-prints in the dark earth, that's what they looked like, before I caught them on the spading fork and shook off the dirt. I had already filled one bucket from the small patch, which was two by two meters, and was now filling a second.

As I cooked three potatoes for supper, the ducks popped up in my mind again. I looked at the three same-size potatoes in the boiling water and had to shake myself, as if that would help, as if the strange visual impression of the three flying skeletons would fall and crash onto the floor. I turned on the radio to distract my thoughts, but *Swan Lake* was playing. I opened a packet of cured ham that I was going to have with the new potatoes, along with some butter, my favorite meal, but when I took the ham out, I saw that it was almost phosphorescent green in the middle, there was something mother-of-pearlish about it. That wasn't what cured ham should look like. I had nothing else in the fridge that would go with boiled new potatoes; lamb salami would seem wretched, strawberry jam was just wrong, and I had only liver paste for the cat. I put the plate of three boiled potatoes down on the table, I had even put on a clean tablecloth, to mark the start of the new potato season, and I had thought of sitting down to drink juice and eat new potatoes and cured ham and butter as I watched the sun move across the sky.

But the three new potatoes on the plate were now swimming in yellow butter, they were somehow transformed, and I couldn't even swallow a mouthful.

Then, out of nowhere, I saw Åsta tottering up the hill toward me. It wasn't difficult to see that the hill was a challenge for her now, she used her stick a bit like an ice pick and hacked her way up, until she was at the house. She knocked on the windowpane and I waved her in. Oh, were you eating, Åsta said. I'm not really hungry after all, I said. Oh, Åsta said, are they new potatoes? Yes, I said. If you'd like them, just help yourself, I haven't used the fork. Thank you very much, said Åsta, and then she gobbled up the three new potatoes faster than I knew it was possible for a person to eat new potatoes, no matter how much butter they had on them. The real reason I came, said Åsta, was that I saw three dead ducks in the sky today. Oh, I said. Yes, Åsta said, they flew straight over my head with a whistling sound. You don't say, I said, because I didn't want to say that I'd seen them as well. If I said that I'd seen them, it would make the dead ducks alive once and for all, as they would not have shown themselves only to me. Åsta had no imagination, she'd never had any imagination, but if she'd seen them, then I had also seen them. I wonder what it means, Åsta said. I'm sure it means nothing, I said. Of course it does, said Åsta. That's why I came to see you, you know about things, she said, and nodded at my bookshelf.

I've never read anything about dead ducks in the sky, I said, so I'm afraid I know nothing. But you could take a guess, Åsta said, you could guess some meaning or another? No, I said, and could hear that it sounded terse. I think, I said, the fact that you saw the ducks means that you do actually have some imagination after all, and you should be happy, here you are, ninety years old, and you've said all your life that the only thing that means anything is what exists here on earth, and now you've seen that there is an afterlife as well. Puh, Åsta said. She didn't look happy. It's true, I said. Now all I wanted was for the cat to come and eat a little liver paste, I wanted to see an animal today, a living animal. I went over to the veranda door, opened it, put some liver paste down on the slab outside, and then called: Puss? Puss? Puss? Puss?

SECONDS

What good are burning fingers, when it said on the packet you'd get a warmer heart!

What good are Baudelaire's burning eyes, when it said on the packet you'd get glossy hair!

What good is this burning conscience, when it said on the packet you'd experience great inner peace, "like an endless ocean"?

What good are these matches, and this dry hay?

No one's going to come here and tell me to set it alight.

Packet: I refuse to read your instructions.

NOTES

"The Thread 3" cites the Norwegian translation by Leiv Heggstad of the Icelandic saga *Egilssoga*, Det Norske Samlaget, 2008 (translated from the Norwegian into English by Kari Dickson).

"Evil Flowers" refers to Charles Baudelaire's *Flowers of Evil*, as translated by Anthony Mortimer, Alma Classics, Alma Books Ltd., 2016.

The photograph in "A Bit Like This" was taken by Étienne Carjat. Credit: David Hunter McAlpin Fund, 1964 / Metropolitan Museum of Art, New York.

"Protest" quotes from the poem "The Galilee Hitch-Hiker" by Richard Brautigan, from *Trout Fishing in America, The Pill versus the Springhill Mine Disaster, and In Watermelon Sugar*, Houghton Mifflin, 1989.

"Escape" is a rewritten version of the foreword to the catalog *Pictures of the Year 2019* (ed. Christian Belgaux), Press Photographers' Association, 2020. The photograph that is described was taken by Therese Jægtvig.

"The Cliffs, When Dead" cites *To the Lighthouse* by Virginia Woolf, Vintage Classics, 2019.

"The Mational Nuseum" quotes from the poem "New Year 1970" by Olav H. Hauge, *Dikt i samling*, Samlaget, 2008 (in translation by Kari Dickson).

"The Nordics Seen from the Outside" quotes from *alphabet* by Inger Christensen, translated by Susanna Nied, New Directions, New York, 2000.

"By the Shack" quotes from *Light, Grass, and Letter in April* by Inger Christensen, translated by Susanna Nied, New Directions, New York, 2011.

"By the Shack" was previously printed in *Kritiker* #53–53 (ed. Julia Wiedlocha and Benjamin Yazdan), 2019.

"A Visit to Monk's House" quotes from *The Waves* by Virginia Woolf, Grafton, 1987.

A NOTE ABOUT THE AUTHOR

Gunnhild Øyehaug is an award-winning Norwegian poet, essayist, and fiction writer. Her story collection *Knots* was published by FSG in 2017, followed in 2018 by *Wait, Blink*, which was adapted into the acclaimed film *Women in Oversized Men's Shirts*, and in 2022 by *Present Tense Machine*. Øyehaug lives in Bergen, where she teaches creative writing.

A NOTE ABOUT THE TRANSLATOR

Kari Dickson was born in Edinburgh, Scotland, and grew up bilingual. She has a BA in Scandinavian studies and an MA in translation. Her translation of *Brown*, written by Håkon Øvreås and illustrated by Øyvind Torseter, won the 2020 Mildred L. Batchelder Award. Before becoming a translator, she worked in theater in London and Oslo. She teaches in the Scandinavian studies department at the University of Edinburgh.